Cont[ents]

CHRISTIAN BROTHERS,
PRIMARY SCHOOL,
DRIMNAGH CASTLE,
DUBLIN 12.

To Caroline, with thanks
for the idea

Dublín Baile Átha Cliath
Walkinstown Branch
Tel. 4550159

1

An amazing find

Edward walked alone, through the park. He walked through the park, not because that was the quickest way home, but because it was forbidden. 'Unless there are at least four of you!' Mrs Rudge warned them, in Assembly. 'And then stay close together. You all know why.'

It was because of the Strangers, of course. Strangers liked hanging about in parks, it was their favourite sort of place. They lurked in parks, waiting to catch unwary children, and take them away, and do unexplained bad things to them. Edward, however, had nothing but scorn for people who were afraid of Strangers.

Strangers were cunning, and crafty, of course, but not as cunning and crafty as Edward Lawson! Just let some Stranger try it on, just let him try!

'Oh look!' Edward would say, pointing at the sky. 'There's a UFO!' And while the Stranger was looking, Edward would be shinning up a tree, quick as lightning, up to the very top, where the Stranger would be too big and heavy to follow. 'Ha, ha!' he would crow at the Stranger. 'Tricked you that time! Dum-dum! Egg-face! Slime-bag!' He would sit safely in his tree, calling down all the rude names he could think of, until, shamed by the insults, the Stranger slunk away in defeat.

Anyway, today there were no Strangers around.

1

Indeed, at this moment, there was no one around at all in this part of the park. Over by the swings there would be mothers with toddlers; here there were only birds, hopping over the hot summer grass, and a grey squirrel or two, darting shyly amongst the branches.

Wait a minute, though, wait a minute, Edward thought – what was that? Way ahead, down by that seat, where the trees to the left of the path were tall and close together, *that* was someone! Someone coming towards him. Someone who suddenly changed course and dived into the shadow of the trees.

Why?

Edward's heart began to beat faster. His steps slowed, and then stopped. Perhaps that *was* a Stranger. Hiding behind a thick trunk, all ready to pounce on him as he passed! Now that it seemed likely he might really be attacked, here in this lonely place, he felt his knees to be, annoyingly, quite weak.

He wouldn't run, though, he wouldn't do that. He'd never respect himself again if he ran, would he? No, he'd do his plan the way he'd worked it out.

A tree. He needed a tree.

Well, there were plenty of trees; there was no shortage of trees in this park. The question was – how was a person supposed to climb one? Now he came to notice it, he realised that if he stood on tiptoe, if he jumped, even, there was no way he could reach even the lowest branch.

Edward turned and, bony legs flying, pounded back the way he had just come. Out of breath, he glanced fearfully over his shoulder. Nothing. Nothing on the path behind him, but far to his right, someone had come out of the trees and was stumbling across the grass and away from him. Up a slope, and over the brow of the little hill, the hunched up figure of Edward's Stranger. Only it didn't look much like a Stranger now, it looked like a girl in trousers, a girl in a big hurry ...

Relief and shame tumbled over each other, a jumble of feelings in Edward's thumping chest. With the back of one hand, he wiped at the sweat which was snaking down the bridge of his nose, and making for his jaw in two tickly channels. He hadn't been afraid really, he told himself, not *really*. He would have climbed that tree if it had been possible, he *would*.

Well, all right, he made a mistake; that was nothing, was it? Anyone could make a mistake about a tree. He would have to make a different plan, that's all. *Then*, let a real stranger come along; just let one come along then!

Edward walked on, feeling in his trouser pocket as he went. In his trouser pocket were today's takings, something reassuring, something to help him feel good about himself.

Three pounds twenty. Only one pound twenty profit, of course, but not bad for five minutes' work! Easy money and a brilliant idea that no one else had thought of. You were allowed to bring apples and crisps for playtime, but plenty of people forgot, and didn't have the chance to buy anything on the way to school because they were being brought by car. Edward, on the other hand, living near and being old enough to come by himself,

3

had ample chance to visit the corner shop which called itself a supermarket. There you could buy multi-packet bags of crisps, and bags of apples – small ones. Then you could open the bags, and sell the items, separately. You could do it behind the toilets, where the teacher on playground duty couldn't see. If the teacher saw, she would certainly be spoilsport enough to stop it; adults were like that. But so far he hadn't got caught, and the number of Edward's customers was growing in the most satisfactory way.

He intended to be a millionaire by the time he was twenty. Only nine years to achieve this goal, but at least he had made a start. Edward smiled to himself, contemplating his happy future. He hummed a little tune. The world was a delightful place, full of sparkling promise.

He was passing the park seat when an odd little sound made him stop again. A mewing sound, like a kitten or something. There was a kitten stuck somewhere, perhaps. Edward looked around for it.

The sound came again.

Under the seat. The sound was coming from under the seat.

But under the seat was only a large, stiff, brown paper carrier bag; someone's rubbish, Edward supposed, that they couldn't be bothered to put in the bin.

Only this bag was moving!

Oh, the kitten must be *inside* the bag. What a funny thing! Edward bent, reached under the seat, and was just about to pick it up when the bag rustled and moved again. Edward drew back his hand. Wait a minute, Edward Lawson, wait a

4

minute. Suppose it's something dangerous inside the bag! A rat, perhaps, or a snake . . . ! No, not a rat, something bigger than a rat . . . a baby crocodile, perhaps, with rows and rows of needle-sharp teeth, and jaws that go *snap*, as they bite your hand off!

Best leave the bag where it is.

On the other hand, how am I going to respect myself if I do any such a wimpish thing?

Edward took a deep breath, picked up the bag, and looked to see what was inside.

There was some hair, not very much, wet and plastered to an otherwise bald little dome. There was a small crumpled face, with screwed up eyes and a mouth that cried weakly. No doubt about it, this was a real live baby!

Astonished, Edward sat on the seat with the bag and the baby on his knees. The baby cried again, and Edward peered more deeply into the bag. The tiny body was wrapped in a clean pink towel, which bulged and shifted here and there. Edward thought the baby was very ugly; perhaps that was why its owner didn't want it. He held it gingerly, not too close.

What was he supposed to do with it? Clearly the baby had been thrown away – what do you do with babies that get thrown away?

It was always happening, of course, you heard about it on the television all the time. People leave babies in dustbins, and in telephone boxes, and someone finds them and takes them to the hospital. 'You're a nuisance though,' he told this baby. 'I don't want to be bothered going to the hospital with you, I want to get home and play with my computer.'

I could take it home and give it to Grandma, of course. Grandma could take it to the hospital, I wouldn't have to waste any more of my time. Or I might meet a policeman on the way. The policeman would be pleased with me for finding the baby, wouldn't he? He might even give me a reward.

Hang about, though, hang about, don't be in too much hurry, Edward Lawson, there might be a better idea. Ha, ha, there is a better idea! That policeman might be too mean to give me a reward. There's a certainer way to make some money here – what about the people who *buy* babies! They do buy them, they do, I saw that on the television as well. They go all the way to other countries, and spend out thousands of pounds, just to buy a baby.

And the thing is, *I've* got one they could buy!

I wouldn't ask them for thousands of pounds, I could let them have it cheap. They could give me five hundred, or six hundred, or ... anyway, not thousands ... Well, perhaps *one* thousand ... It would still be a bargain because they wouldn't have to pay for the aeroplane to go to that other country ...

Excitement mounting, Edward peeped into the bag again. It's not *really* all that ugly, he thought, not really ... I expect some people would think it was quite pretty ... Well, all right, I could let them have it a bit cheap considering how ugly it is, that would be fair, wouldn't it?

The future was not just sparkling now, it was a great golden blaze, shimmering and wonderful, and just within his reach. Not in nine years' time, not in five years, or four, but *now*.

There were people coming along the path towards him now, he saw them out of the corner of his eye. Not Strangers, just a few slowcoaches of parents, choosing this way to escort their children home. Quickly, Edward stuffed the baby in the bag back under the seat, and took his homework out of his school bag, so he could pretend to be doing it until they had passed. Giddy with exhilaration, he forced his mind to deal with the practicalities of his new future.

There are a few problems, he acknowledged. Like – I'd have to keep the baby somewhere. Till I find someone who wants to buy it, I'd have to keep it somewhere. That is one problem.

. . . And feed it, and all that sort of thing. That is another problem, because I don't really know how to do it.

And keep the whole thing a secret, because they won't let me if they find out. The adults won't let me, they'll say the baby has to go to the hospital, I know them. And it's not fair because it's my baby, I found it!

Looks like I'll have to find someone to help me. Who? Well, a girl of course! Girls know about babies. I must hurry up and find a girl, before they all get home.

Eagerly, Edward dragged the bag with the baby in it out from under the seat once more. The baby seemed to have gone to sleep. His school bag over one shoulder, and the paper bag dangling from one hand, Edward hurried to the park gate – and hesitated. Of course he would have to give this girl some of the money, and that was a pity . . . Never mind, he wouldn't have to give her much. She could be, like, his servant or something. After all it was his baby, he found it.

He looked carefully up and down the road. There was one girl from his class, and one from the other Year Six class, but they were both with their mums, or other people's mums, and with younger brothers and sisters tagging along. He wanted one by herself.

There! What about that one! Alice Cousins, what about her? A most uninteresting person – so quiet in class you might miss her altogether. But she must be sensible. She must be sensible, because you couldn't help noticing how Miss Churchwood was always picking her for doing important jobs. And whatever she was asked to do she always did it. And, *and . . . she had a new baby brother,* didn't she . . . or a sister, or something! So she'd be sure to know all about babies.

Pity she had to be with her friend, that scatty Miranda person. Perhaps Miranda could be got rid of.

Edward ran, calling Alice's name.

The short, lumpy girl with the heavy red face stopped and looked back. 'What is it?' She spoke in a small shy voice, her eyes not quite meeting his. There was no expression on her face – there hardly ever was.

'Come back here a minute, I want to ask you something.'

She came, obediently, and the other girl came too.

'Not you!' Edward told her. 'Alice.'

8

'Not *me*?' Miranda's smooth blonde hair swung, a cascade of gold as she tipped her head sideways. She favoured Edward with a teasing smile; the green eyes with their long lashes sparkled. Silly cow, Edward thought scornfully, she thinks I fancy her! All the boys did fancy Miranda a bit, he knew, all except for him. Edward fancied no one because he was never going to get married, ever. Catch him sharing his millions, no way!

'I want to talk to Alice, all right?' he said. 'It's private, and it's a secret.'

Miranda linked arms with the other girl. 'Alice is my friend,' she insisted. 'We don't have secrets from each other, do we, Alice? We tell each other everything, don't we?'

Alice agreed. She would, of course. She was an agreeing sort of person.

Edward sighed. 'OK, you as well then, but you have to swear not to tell anybody. Both of you.'

'Yeah, yeah, we both swear, don't we, Alice? Hurry up, then, what's the secret?'

Edward held the bag open. 'Look!'

Miranda screamed. 'Oh, the angel! Oh, the sweet little thing!'

'Shut up!' Edward hissed. 'We don't want people to notice!'

'Why? Whose baby is it?'

'Mine, of course, I found it. Somebody threw it away, and I found it, under a seat in the park.'

'It's newborn,' said Alice. 'You should take it to the hospital, or the police station.'

'It would be more fun to keep it though, wouldn't it?' Edward pointed out. 'But the thing is, I can't actually look after a baby all by myself.'

9

'Well, we'll help you!' Miranda enthused. 'We'll help you, won't we, Alice?' She began jumping up and down with excitement. 'Oh the angel! Oh, the lovely little thing!'

If she says that one more time, Edward thought, I shall probably hit her. And I can't mention about selling the baby now she's gone all soppy about it. With an effort, he controlled his annoyance. 'The thing is,' he said, 'we have to think of somewhere to keep it.'

'It will need bottles, and nappies,' said Alice slowly. 'And it will have to be bathed, and somewhere warm to sleep because they mustn't catch cold . . . It ought to go to the hospital really.'

'Oh, not the *hospital*,' said Miranda. 'Not the hospital, Alice! It's all right, Edward, we're not taking the darling, darling thing to the hospital . . . Can I hold it a minute?'

'No . . . I mean, only if you help. If you think of somewhere we can keep it.'

' . . . What about my bedroom?'

'Get real!'

'Well – *I* don't know, do I? Edward, *please* let me hold the darling, darling baby!' Miranda put her head on one side and gave him her most charming smile. 'Please, pretty please, with sugar on top!'

'Only if—'

'*I* know,' said Miranda, suddenly. 'What about your playhouse, Alice?'

Alice just looked wooden; you couldn't tell from her face what she was thinking or feeling. 'It wouldn't do,' she said, in her small shy voice. 'I'm sorry.'

'It *would* do! Why wouldn't it? Your playhouse – right down the bottom of the garden, it's perfect!'

'It wouldn't do,' Alice said again.

'Yes, it would! Why wouldn't it? Nobody ever goes there, only us.'

'They do sometimes. When they want to fetch me for something.'

'Well, they don't have to see what's inside! You're just being difficult, isn't she, Edward?'

Alice turned her head. 'We ought to take the baby to the hospital, though.'

'Oh, fiddle the hospital! I'm tired of hearing about the boring old hospital, aren't you, Edward? Come on, Alice! Please, Alice! Please pretty please with sugar on top! You're nodding, I saw her nodding, didn't you, Edward? You can't get out of it now. She can't get out of it now, can she? So let's just go, and I can hold the dear, darling, sweet, lovely little baby; I can't wait!'

2

Lies and more lies

Alice's head spun, floating oddly somewhere above her body. This wasn't real, it couldn't be real, and yet it was! And what was going to happen now?

Clearly, what she had said yes to was a very wrong and silly thing to do, and Mum and Dad would not be pleased with her if they found out. And how could they *not* find out if this wrong and silly thing went on for any length of time? And then they would be really shocked and angry, wouldn't they? Mum hardly ever got angry, but Dad did sometimes, and he would surely be angry about this! Her parents would punish her, she supposed, but that was not the worst thing. The worst thing was how unpleased they were going to be.

On the other hand, if she had said no, then *Miranda* would not be pleased. And Miranda was her best friend in all the world. Alice loved Miranda, was desperately proud of being best friends with her; she couldn't bear it if that ever came to an end.

It was so hard to please everyone, all the time; but when you weren't pretty, or clever, that was the only way to make sure of being liked, and wanted, wasn't it? And besides, pleasing people gave you a happy feeling, inside.

Number 25 Almond Avenue. And oh dear, there was Mum on the lawn, stretched out in a sun-lounger, a baby's pram beside her. Mum opened her eyes lazily as the children tried to tiptoe past her. 'Hullo, you lot – where are you off to?'

Alice felt herself turn cold with guilt and fear, in spite of the hot sun. 'Just down to the playhouse.' Proud of her pretty mother as Alice was, she fervently wished her elsewhere at that moment.

Alice's mother smiled a sleepy smile. 'Lovely day, isn't it?' She had a high-pitched, fluting sort of voice. 'Hullo, Miranda. And ... er ... whatever your name is.' She smoothed the flowing blue and purple Indian dress over her slender legs, and smiled another sleepy smile.

'We're going to the playhouse,' Alice said again. She forced herself not to look at Edward's carrier bag. If she didn't look, then perhaps Mum wouldn't look.

'Just run down to the shop for me first, there's a good girl. You don't mind, do you?'

Alice swallowed the lump of dismay which had risen in her throat and was threatening to choke her. 'What about my friends?'

Alice's mother smiled again. 'Come on now, you can all go, can't you? It's only that I'm out of eggs. Won't take you more than ten minutes! Leave your school bags here.'

What's wrong with *her* going, Edward thought furiously. She looks like she's been lying there all afternoon – why does Alice have to do it? He felt a slight movement in the carrier bag which dangled against his legs. He held the bag behind his back, where he felt it moving some more.

'What have you got there?' said Alice's mother

13

to Edward. She turned her head, mildly curious. 'Looks like something alive.'

'It's a kitten,' said Edward. 'I found it in the park.'

'Oh, let me see.' She eased herself up slowly, and leaned forward.

'Better not,' said Miranda. 'It's a really horrid kitten. It scratches. And it bit Edward, didn't it, Edward?'

'Yes, it did. That's why I put it in the bag. So it can't bite any more.'

'Ugh! How not very nice! You should have a tetanus jab for that.'

'Oh, it's OK.'

'Well, I don't agree. Better safe than sorry.'

'I mean,' said Edward desperately, 'it's OK because I had a jab already. Last week, when another cat bit me.'

'Ho, hum . . . Well please take this one away. Ugh! And don't bring it back!' Alice's mother turned her back on Edward and his kitten, to smile fondly into the pram.

'All right, I won't. I mean, I won't bring it back. I'll take it away now.' Edward hurried back to the road, glad to have escaped but with no idea what he was going to do with the baby now.

Miranda ran after him. 'Look, we don't have to give up,' she said. 'We can still sneak the baby into Alice's playhouse, after we did the shopping. Can't we, Alice?'

Alice was trailing behind, the wooden expression on the heavy red face, only her dragging footsteps showing how unhappy she really was.

'Can't we?' Miranda insisted.

'How long could we keep it for, though?' Alice struggled to say. 'Even if we can get it in? I mean – it's not very sensible, is it? I mean . . . I'm sorry . . .'

'Oh, why does everything have to be *sensible*? Come on, Alice, it's fun!'

Well, he'd wanted someone sensible to help him, Edward reflected. Not that sensible, though. What was the matter with this Alice, she wasn't *trying* to help! Anyway, he wasn't giving up now, he most certainly wasn't. 'We have to find a way to sneak past Alice's mum,' he said.

Let them *not* think of anything, Alice prayed. Let them not think of a way round the problem, and we won't have to go on with this silly wrong thing, and it won't be because of me, it will be because of just bad luck!

'I know!' said Miranda. 'The baby can be my doll! We can throw the bag away, and the baby can be my doll that I just fetched from my house, how about that?'

Nice one, Miranda! Edward gave Miranda a condescending look of approval, but Alice began to think how lovely it would be to start this day all over again – only this time have just safe, easy, ordinary things in it.

The shop was cool, and smelled of safe, ordinary things. Alice breathed the comforting, reassuring smells, and tried not to think about Edward and Miranda, left outside with the baby, where the heat was making sticky pools of black tar, on the pavement.

'Now you *have* to let me hold it,' said Miranda

15

eagerly. 'You have to let me hold it now, Edward, so we can pretend it's my doll.'

She lifted it out of the bag, covering its head and face with her hand. The baby began to cry. There were people in the road; surely someone must notice, and think something peculiar was going on. 'Do something!' said Edward, urgently.

'Like what?'

'Stop it crying, of course.'

'Well, I don't know how to do that, do I? You can't expect me to know everything!'

Frantic with anxiety, Edward felt his temper erupt, spilling unreasonably all over Miranda. 'So what's the use of you? You silly, stupid, useless cow! What's the use of you?'

Miranda stared at him in astonishment. She was not accustomed to having boys speak to her like that. Haughtily she thrust the baby at Edward. 'All right, you wonderful useful know-it-all person, *you* do it!'

He took the baby, because there seemed no choice, and by some miracle it did stop crying. He pulled the towel over its head and held it awkwardly in his arms. One passer-by did turn to look. 'He likes playing with dolls,' Miranda gleefully informed the passer-by. 'Funny, isn't it? He's always been like that!'

Edward hated her. At that moment he thought he had probably never hated anyone so much in his whole life.

Alice came out of the shop. 'Do have a look at Edward! Playing with his doll!' Miranda doubled up, exploding with malicious laughter.

'If you don't stop saying that,' Edward

threatened her, 'you're going to get a fat lip, all right?'

He looked all set to give her one, all set to forget the baby altogether; in her alarmed imagination Alice saw the baby crashing to the ground, disregarded, even trampled on! She threw her shopping down, and took the baby from Edward's unresisting arms. Shaking inwardly with fright, Alice held the tiny bundle close, cradling its head against her shoulder.

And that was when the feeling came.

It was a feeling so strong, so unexpected, that it left her standing in bewilderment, unable to grasp the meaning of it – until she found herself thinking the words: I want this baby to be mine! Oh, I *want* it, I want it to be *mine*!

Edward sulked, kicking his heel against the wall behind him. 'Come on,' Miranda coaxed him. 'Cheer up, I didn't mean it!'

Edward went on kicking his heel against the wall.

'I was only teasing,' said Miranda. 'Come on, we'll let Alice carry the doll, I mean the baby, shall we?' She picked up the shopping and Edward went on kicking at the wall.

'All right,' said Miranda, 'you just stay there if you want to, Edward. Alice and I can look after the baby by ourselves, you don't have to be in it!'

With a great effort, Edward swallowed his pride and his anger. If he let the baby out of his sight at this point, he could lose his claim to it. He stopped kicking the wall. 'Yes I do have to be in it. It's my baby, I found it!'

17

'Well come on, then,' said Miranda. 'We're wasting all the afternoon.'

Back once more, round the side of Alice's house, where Alice's mother once more lay in the sun, now idly and contentedly rocking the pram with one foot. 'One of the eggs got broken,' said Alice, with some apprehension.

'Ho, hum, just leave them in the kitchen,' said her mother.

She didn't even bother to ask what happened. She's not really interested in anything I do, Alice thought, with a stab of hurt in spite of her relief. She's only interested in William now. I think Dad's only interested in William now, as well, not me. There was the smell of new-mown grass. Dad had mown the lawn yesterday evening, she remembered, and she had helped him willingly, clipping away at the edges until her back ached. But afterwards Dad had gone straight upstairs to watch William being bathed, and forgotten all about her.

The playhouse used to be the garden shed; but there was a bigger one now, much nearer the house, so when Alice asked if it was possible, if they really didn't want it for something else, if, perhaps, if they were *sure*, could it be possible for her to have the old one for her private place . . . they said yes, why not – a bit surprised to be asked, because Alice hardly ever asked for anything.

They assumed she wanted it for dolls' parties, and for dressing up – which she did, of course – but it was also wonderful because you could do all sorts of interesting secret things in your very own private place.

You could dress up all by yourself, where no one

18

could see you doing it and think how silly you were. You could pretend to be people out of books, you could write your own stories and hide them away where no one could laugh at the bad spellings and the funny ideas.

Best of all you could act out being a nurse, in a children's hospital, which was the thing you wanted to be more than anything, one day, only you were afraid you might not be clever enough to pass the exams.

Of course, you couldn't tell anyone about your secret things. And if they asked, as they sometimes did, what you had been doing down there all alone, you couldn't always be exactly truthful, because you were shy of letting people see your inside self.

And anyway, there were better things to do after last Christmas, when Miranda came to live at Number 29 – only two doors away. After that Alice's private place was Miranda's private place as well, where Alice and Miranda always did Miranda's things – trying out different hair styles, experimenting with make-up 'borrowed' from Miranda's sister, making fun jewellery, and endless gossiping about people at school. And if Alice wasn't terribly interested in these activities, she was happy to pretend that she was. Likewise, if Miranda suddenly lost interest in what they were doing and wanted to do something else, then Alice was happy to go along with that too. Anything to keep Miranda wanting to be her best friend.

All that was happiness – but this, this was something else! Oh, how could Alice have wished this day not to have happened! It was the best, the most thrilling day of her life so far. However it all ended, whatever trouble there might be, about today Alice was glad, glad, *glad*.

Inside the playhouse, Miranda held out her arms for the baby. 'My turn again now,' she claimed.

Carefully, Alice handed the little bundle over; it was a wrench to let it go. 'You have to hold its head,' she warned. 'It can't hold its own head up yet.'

'Don't forget it's my baby,' said Edward. He was glad to see that Alice seemed properly keen now, on the idea of looking after it.

'Oh the darling, darling, sweet little precious! Oh, I love it to bits!' squealed Miranda.

'Don't forget it's my baby, though,' said Edward, again.

'Shall we find out if it's a girl or a boy?' Alice suggested.

Miranda giggled. 'That's a good idea!' She began to unwrap the towel. The baby threw back one arm, and its mouth puckered into a yawn. The tiny hand opened and closed, clutching at the air. 'Boy,' said Miranda.

Edward was not interested. Boy or girl, what did it matter, as long as someone would buy it.

'Oh, look!' said Miranda. 'It's got a funny sort of thing sticking out of its tummy.'

Edward peered to see. 'There's something wrong with it!' he exclaimed in dismay. What a nuisance! Who would want a baby with a funny sort of thing sticking out of its tummy?

'That's nothing,' said Alice. 'That's meant to be there. It will come off by itself in a few days, and his belly button will be underneath.'

'Are you sure?'

'My brother's was just like that.'

'Oh, right.' Edward's spirits soared. Everything was coming right now. The boring part taken care of, and nothing for him to concern himself with but the real point of it all, the money! He couldn't wait to get on with that; there were plans to be made, and no time to be lost, very likely. 'I might as well be off, then,' he said.

'Really!' said Miranda. 'After all that fuss?'

'I've got things to do at home,' Edward explained, at the door.

I don't like Edward, Alice thought. He doesn't love the baby at all. He doesn't even seem interested now. 'Fancy Edward just going, like that,' she commented.

'Who cares?' said Miranda. 'Oh the sweet little darling . . . What shall we call him, Alice?'

'I don't know. We can think about that after. We have to find him somewhere to sleep first. And some milk. And I think he should have a bath . . .'

'Mmmm – you lovely little thing, you! You want some nice milk, don't you?'

Alice was looking round the little playhouse. That doll's pram in the corner, that would do for now. There was a blanket in it, and a pillow, but they were too grubby for a real baby. Real babies had to have bedding that was spotlessly clean, otherwise they might breathe some germs, and the germs could make them ill. 'I shall have to get some stuff from the house,' she told Miranda. 'I shall have to get some of William's stuff . . . Somehow.'

Miranda kissed the baby fervently on the top of

his head. She wrinkled her nose. 'He's a bit mucky, isn't he?'

'Well that's what I mean. He has to be bathed and all sorts . . .'

Alice's head had begun to float again. What was happening to her – was she turning into someone else? How could she be planning something so wrong, and deceitful, and not even feeling too guilty about it, any more? She struggled to control the floating, so she could think more clearly about what had to be done, and an idea began to form. 'You will have to help me,' she said.

'All right. I'll hold the baby while you get the things.'

'I know you want to go on holding the baby, I know that, Miranda. The thing is, though, we can't keep him if we don't have the things to look after him with . . . I'm sorry . . . you will have to put him down for a bit and go and talk to my mum. If she isn't asleep. And stop her coming in the kitchen, so she doesn't see what I'm doing . . . I'm sorry . . .'

Miranda wrinkled her nose, then beamed. 'OK, that'll be fun.'

'There'll be other things to do after that, that's only the first bit . . . I'm sorry.'

'OK, it's all fun. You don't have to be sorry, just tell me what you want me to do, and I'll do it.'

There was nowhere to put the baby except the doll's pram, spread with the grubby blanket; at least the pink and white towel looked clean. Miranda led the way to the house, skipping and giggling. 'The first thing is to get a feed for him,' said Alice, plodding along behind. 'He's asleep now, but he's sure to be hungry soon, and when that happens he'll cry and cry and cry. The feed is in the kitchen, and the bottles. You will have to keep my mum out of the way. For about five minutes.'

'No problem!' said Miranda.

Alice's mother was in the kitchen already. 'Just run up and get a fresh nappy for me,' she said to Alice. 'There's a good girl. You know where they are.'

'Are you going to change William?' said Miranda.

'However did you guess!'

Miranda laughed, obligingly. 'Where are you going to do it?'

'*Where*? What a funny question!'

'I mean – can I watch?'

'If you like.' Alice's mother was doing something with warm water and a bottle and some powder out of a tin. 'He has to have his feed first.'

'It's a lovely day,' Miranda coaxed. 'Wouldn't it be nice to give him his feed in the garden?'

'Well, of course – I was going to, anyway.'

'Oh, good!'

Miranda and Alice's mum sat side by side on the terrace bench, their finely shaped features and long fair hair making the two of them look very much like mother and daughter. Indeed, Alice's mother could not help wishing, sometimes, that her own daughter *was* just a little bit more like Miranda. Alice was a good girl, of course, a great help around the house and with the baby; a good kid always – but it would have been nice if she was prettier, and had a bit of sparkle to her . . . Alice's mother turned her attention to William, her pride and joy. 'Oh, look!' said Miranda, suddenly.

'What? Where?'

'A great big hairy spider, just ran over my leg!'

'Ugh! How not very nice! Anyway, it's gone now . . . What's Alice going down the path for?'

'*I* don't know. I suppose she wanted something from the playhouse.'

'Couldn't it have waited? I asked her to get a fresh nappy for William.'

'He's got a rash.'

'*What?*'

'There. Look. William's got all spots down the side of his face.'

'Where?'

'There!'

'*Miranda!* What's wrong with your eyes? He's got no more of a rash than you have.'

'There's something on his arm, then.'

'Where? That? That's a little birthmark. He's always had it.'

'Oh. I thought it might be menin— You know, menin—'

'Meningitis?' Alice's mother laughed a little fluting laugh. 'Look at him, Miranda! He's as healthy as ever he could be. Aren't you, my poppet? Oh, there's a smile! William's first ever smile! What date is it? What's the date, I have to write it in his book.'

Miranda screamed and clutched her knee.

'What's the matter now?'

'Oh, it hurts! It hurts!'

'*What* hurts?'

'I think a wasp stung me.'

'Ugh! Take your hand away. Let me see!'

'I can't, it hurts too much.'

'Well, I can't do anything about it if you won't let me look, can I? Where's Alice got to? Oh, *there* you are! What have you been running up and down the garden for?'

Alice's heavy cheeks were redder than ever, and she seemed out of breath. 'I'm sorry . . . Here's the nappy . . . I'm sorry . . .' She floundered; she stood stiff and rigid, struggling not to betray her confusion. 'I just . . .'

Miranda began moaning and rocking. 'My wasp sting! It hurts, it hurts!'

Alice's mother was busily changing William. 'Oh, for heaven's sake you see to her, Alice! There's some stuff in the bathroom called After-bite, I think . . . Or you could go home, Miranda, and get your mother to do it.'

Miranda stood up suddenly. 'I have to go home anyway, I nearly forgot.'

'Must you?' said Alice, in dismay that was something like panic.

'I have to . . . I have to clean out the rabbits. And it's my ballet class, I have to have my tea early. I nearly forgot. We'll play – you know, that game – we'll play that game again tomorrow.'

Alice swallowed. 'All right.'

'*And* I have to do my homework,' Miranda added, running to pick up her school bag from the lawn.

Alice swallowed again, trying not to feel resentful about being so badly let down. Of *course* Miranda had to see to her rabbits, and go to her ballet class, of *course* she did! 'It's all right, you go.'

She turned slowly, and began plodding back to the playhouse.

'Alice!' her mother called. 'I want you to find William's book for me.'

'I don't think she can hear you,' said Miranda.

'Ho, hum, later will do ... Who had his first smile today, then?' his mother cooed at William.

'Anyway, my leg's all right now.'

'Oh, a miracle cure,' said Alice's mother, not really listening.

Back in the playhouse, Alice cuddled the baby and tried to coax him with the bottle she had brought. Fear and loneliness closed in on her like a great black cloud. She fought the cloud, willing it to go away.

All right, there was plenty she could do for the baby by herself. She could feed him, and put a nappy on him; she had a small store of those now, as well as the feed. She couldn't bath him, though, there hadn't been time to organise that, and without Miranda to distract Mum's attention, she didn't see how she was going to manage it. She would have to get up in the middle of the night it looked like. When everyone was asleep. She would have to get up and find something. A washing-up bowl would do. And some warm water. And one of William's blankets.

Lucky it was a hot day. Lucky there had been hot nights just lately so the baby wouldn't catch cold ...

It wasn't wrong to keep this baby, was it ... Not really ... Well, all right, it was wrong in a way, but she wasn't going to let herself think about that, she

26

was only going to think about how wonderful it was to have something like this of her very own!

You're *mine*, she thought. You're *my* baby.

Because he *was* just hers, wasn't he? He was hers because she was the one that was looking after him, and she was the one that really loved him.

First Edward had gone, and then Miranda, Alice thought. They had left her to look after the baby all by herself. And anyway, they had other things. Miranda had her rabbits and her ballet lessons, and something called speech and drama, as well; and they were clearly more important to her than the baby. Edward had his money-making thing behind the toilets at school, and he'd soon forget all about the baby most likely. If he hadn't forgotten already.

So the baby is mine, Alice thought. He's all mine and nobody else's!

She wasn't going to think about how all this would end. Perhaps it *wouldn't* end, after all. Perhaps there would be a way it could go on and on. Anyway, that's what she was going to think.

As she fastened the baby's nappy he opened his eyes, which were very blue. Alice stroked his palm and felt, to her delight, how the tiny fist closed around her finger. Dreamily, happily, she began to consider names . . .

Oh, but she must go, she must go! William's bath, she nearly forgot! She always helped with William's bath, and it must surely be time for that.

Alice laid her baby in the doll's pram. He was asleep now, fed and nappied; he would be all right for a few hours, she hoped. The pink and white towel he was wrapped in would do for now, and she would be back with a clean blanket just as soon as ever she could. The feeding bottle would have to stay where it was . . .

Reluctantly, she plodded back to the house.

Edward was rather proud of his grandma.

Edward's grandma had straggly hair, and her clothes looked as though they had come out of the dressing-up box, so she didn't look like other people's grandmas at all, and that was fine, because who wanted a grandma that was like everyone else's? Edward's grandma did her own thing – nice one, Grandma!

Edward's grandma was doing her best to take the place of his dead mum, and deep down, in a part of him he wasn't aware of existing, Edward loved her passionately.

She had been doing her best for five years now, and mostly she got it right. For instance, she never hugged or kissed him, because he didn't much care for that sort of thing. But she gave him his space, which was important. She didn't ask questions, she let him be as secretive as he wanted to be. She was always ready to listen, but she never pried.

So this afternoon, when Edward burst into the house and began shouting could he have the *Edge Hill Echo*, Grandma didn't ask him why he wanted it, even though she was reading it herself, at that moment. 'Let me have it back when you've finished,' she said. 'I was just checking up on everybody's stars.'

'Dad says the stars are rubbish.'

'Your dad doesn't know everything.'

28

Edward took the paper to his room, and opened it eagerly at the 'Wanted' page. The scent of fresh newsprint stung his nose with hope as he studied the advertisements that people had sent in, to say what they wanted to buy. There were columns and columns of these. Fridges, cookers, televisions, cameras – didn't *anyone* want to buy a baby? He was slightly cheered, on reading the 'For Sale' column, that no one seemed to have a baby for sale either. That meant his was precious, and might fetch a higher price . . .

Hang about, though, hang about! Careful here. Perhaps it's against the law to sell a baby.

Well, come to think of it, it *must* be against the law, else why do people take babies to the hospital, instead of selling them, like I'm going to? They're afraid of if the police find out, that's what! That's why they go to other countries.

Could I go to prison, if I sold my baby and the police found it out . . . ?

I'm not giving up, I'm not! Not now I've got this far. I'm just going to be very cunning and clever. I don't know how to do it yet, but there must be a way to find out who wants a baby, and still keep it a secret from the police . . .

Anyway, kids don't go to prison, I saw that on the telly as well. Even if they steal cars, and break into houses, they still don't go to prison so I'm quite safe really . . .

I know, I've got it! I'll ask around at school tomorrow. I won't make it obvious, I'm not that silly. I'll just say something like: 'Don't you think it's sad, when somebody wants a baby and they can't get one?' And sooner or later someone will say they know a person like that. And I'll say: 'Oh do you? Who?' And when I have their name and where they live, I can go to their house and do a deal.

Easy peasy!

A mile away, a girl of fifteen and three-quarters called Emily sat watching television with her parents. She was frightened and not feeling very well, and struggling hard not to let her parents see any of this. It was time for the news. Oh please let them say it, Emily begged in her heart. *Please* let them say he's been found!

Nothing. No mention of a newborn baby boy, found under a park seat, and taken to a hospital to be looked after.

Could he still be there, under the park seat? Might he be there all night? The thought was too dreadful to bear. Emily pushed it away and tried to concentrate on how the worst was over now. All those months of wearing loose clothes, and hiding her secret, because her parents would surely be angry with her for having a baby when she wasn't supposed to.

And she'd had it all by herself, hadn't she, she'd managed that part. All by herself in the bathroom, while her parents were at work. And she'd known what to do, because the book in the library had told her. Only she couldn't keep him, she couldn't look after him, and no one must ever find out, ever!

But why weren't they saying it, on the news, that her baby was safe in the hospital?

Why had she put him under the seat? Why

hadn't she have put him *on* the seat, where someone would have been bound to see him right away? Because she was scared of getting caught, that's why! Because she could see there was someone coming, and she wanted to give herself time to get away . . . But she should have thought of the baby, not herself! She should have put him *on* the seat, she should have put him *on* the seat!

Tomorrow she would go to the park. She would *make* herself go, just to make sure he wasn't still in that bag, under the seat. She would have to miss school again, or be late, but she'd told so many lies just lately, and got away with them, she could surely manage just a few more.

3

Rock-a-bye baby

Alice lay in bed, covered only with a sheet, because the night was so sticky and hot.

She was trying desperately hard to keep awake. She knew her parents had gone to bed, but they couldn't be asleep yet because she could hear their voices. There was Mum's little fluting laugh, and there was Dad's big rumble, rumble, HAW, HAW, HAW! Dad was telling one of his jokey stories. Correction – Dad was telling one jokey story after another. Here it came again – rumble, rumble, HAW, HAW, HAW! A voice as big as Dad himself, and how Dad loved his jokes! Alice loved them as well, usually, only not tonight.

Dad wouldn't find the baby a joke, though. Alice could picture his heavy red face, so like her own, not laughing good-naturedly now, not finding the baby funny at all.

I can't go on calling him *the baby*, she thought. He must have a name.

Now what would suit him? What does he look like? Not an Edward, for certain, and we don't want another William. I know – *Harry*. I'm going to call my baby Harry.

Waves of sleepiness washed over her. She fought against them, but they were too powerful. They washed over and around her, and swept her away, far out, far out, where they tossed her from one muddled dream to another.

She woke with a start.

She wasn't supposed to be sleeping, she was supposed to be doing something important... What? Of course, of course, she was supposed to be seeing to her baby. Her baby! Did she dream that? Was it really true? Yes, it was true, it was true, there was a real live baby hidden in the playhouse! *Harry*... Oh, she must go to him, she must go to him.

The house was very quiet now, the air in the room heavy, and thick with night. Alice slipped out of bed, preparing to feel her way downstairs in the dark. She was frightened, but not as much as she would have expected to be. It was the thought of Harry that worried her mostly – little Harry, all by himself in the playhouse, needing her. I'm coming, she called to him silently, Mummy's coming now.

In the room next door, William began to cry.

Shut up, Alice commanded him in her mind. You're going to wake Mum and Dad.

William cried louder. You nuisance, you nuisance, Alice told him. You're just a nuisance, that's what you are! Ashamed, she amended that thought. I didn't mean it, I do love you really. I *do* love you, it's just that...

There were more sounds from her parents' room. Someone was getting up to attend to William. Alice lay down again, covering herself with the sheet, lying still and silent, so no one would guess she was awake...

Quiet again at last – everyone fast asleep once

more. Alice crept down the stairs in her nighty, her bare feet making no sound on the velvety carpet. In the kitchen, she hesitated; dared she turn on the light? Better not, someone might see. Instead she tugged at the roller blind until it shot up. Outside there was a moon – only a little new one, not very bright, but bright enough for her to see what she was doing. Deftly, she made up a new feed; luckily there was always a supply of freshly boiled water in the spare electric kettle, all ready for William's feeds, that only needed to be warmed slightly when necessary. She must remember to keep the supply topped up, in case Mum noticed, Alice thought. Really, there were *so* many things that would have to be remembered!

She filled the washing-up bowl with hot water. She took two clean tea towels from the drawer and laid them beside the other things while she struggled with the bolt on the back door. The key was no problem, but the bolt was stiff; it hurt her fingers, and when it finally gave, there was a sharp clanging sound.

Alice waited, sweating with fear now, in case Mum or Dad should have heard . . .

Nothing.

Alice went through the kitchen door into the conservatory, where there was another bolt and key to be managed. William's pram was in the conservatory, and she would have liked to take one of his blankets, but decided she would have to come back for that, since she already had enough to carry.

Still on bare feet Alice began her lonely plod down the garden path.

There was a cry. She heard it when she was not much more than halfway to the playhouse – a thin little wail, desperate with need. Alice began a little stumbling run, calling in a hoarse whisper: 'It's all right, Harry darling, I'm coming! Mummy's coming now!'

Inside the playhouse she put the things she had brought on one of the two chairs. She picked Harry out of his doll's pram and sat in the other chair, rocking him and holding him close. He took the bottle willingly this time, sucking thirstily. Now there were two of William's bottles that had to be returned somehow, and sterilised. Anyway, best not think of too many problems at a time.

Leaning forward, Alice carefully tested the temperature of the water in the washing-up bowl. Good – just right! Carefully, gently, she unwrapped the baby and felt his nappy. It was hard to tell if it needed changing, and she couldn't see properly because she was still trying to manage by the little bit of moonlight, coming through the uncurtained window of the playhouse. She'd give him a fresh nappy anyway, to make him all clean and new.

Leaning forward again, she lowered Harry into the bowl and began to slosh the water over him, as she had seen Mum do so many times with William. It was the wrong way round really, she knew, he should have had his bath first; but he had been so hungry, hadn't he, and so much in need of comfort. His tiny limbs threshed the water.

With infinite care, Alice lifted him out and began to dry him with one of the tea towels she had brought. Then she put a clean nappy on him, wrapped him in the other tea towel, and held

35

him close again, rocking and singing 'Sleep baby sleep' to him, in a voice just above a whisper.

It was a shame he had to be wrapped in a tea towel. Perhaps tomorrow she could get him some of William's clothes to wear. The blanket, though! What about the blanket she meant to get from William's pram? And the washing-up bowl at least should be returned, before Mum noticed it had gone. Alice placed her sleeping baby back in his makeshift bed, and began her barefoot journey back to the house.

The washing-up bowl first. Now for the blanket. Really, things were turning out to be not too difficult after all. Perhaps there was an angel or something, watching over her to make sure nothing went wrong.

It was just at this point, when Alice was thinking about the angel, that she blundered into the kitchen table, and knocked over one of the chairs. The falling chair made a dreadful clatter; Alice picked it up and stood with suddenly thudding heart, uncertain what to do now. Surely someone must have heard! But Harry needed his blanket. Already there was a coolness in the air, the coolness that comes towards morning. She listened for footsteps coming from above, but there was nothing . . .

It's because of my angel, Alice thought, wanting to believe it.

She took a deep breath and made for the conservatory again. She bent over William's pram, feeling with her hands. There were two blankets here usually, folded at the end when the weather was hot; surely Mum wouldn't miss one!

She didn't hear him coming through the kitchen, because his feet were as bare as her own, but she felt his big presence just behind her, and let out a terrified scream.

'Blow me down, it's *Alice*!'

And the big voice was Dad's, and the big presence was Dad's, and there was great big Dad in his pyjamas, wielding a heavy table lamp, all ready to attack the 'burglar' who had broken into his home.

'*Alice*! . . . All right, all right, I'm sorry I scared you. But what do you think you're doing? Out here in the middle of the night!'

It was no good – once again she couldn't think of a lie. 'I don't know,' she whispered.

Dad stared at her, then began to laugh. 'HAW, HAW, HAW, I know what it is – you've been sleepwalking!'

' . . . Have I?'

'Well you must have, Pudding, stands to reason. And I went and woke you up – HAW, HAW, HAW – and you're not supposed to do that, are you?'

'It's all right,' said Alice, weakly. 'I don't mind.' At that moment she didn't even mind being called Pudding, though usually she secretly hated it.

'Come on, let's get you back to bed.' He switched on the landing light. 'How about a nice hot drink, eh?'

Mum was leaning over the banisters, not particularly frightened about the 'burglar', having total faith in Dad's ability to cope. 'It's all right,' said Dad. 'Only old Pudding here, sleepwalking. HAW, HAW, HAW!'

'*What?* She's never done that before!'

'Well, she has now . . . I don't suppose it's anything serious, lots of kids do it.'

'Do they? You don't think I need take her to the doctor, then?'

'Nah! Not just for the once.'

'Oh, right.' Mum smiled her lazy smile. 'That's good, because I have to take William to the clinic tomorrow morning and I don't see how I could manage both.'

'Take William to the clinic?' There was alarm in Dad's voice now. 'What's wrong with him?'

'Nothing – just his check-up.'

'Oh, ah, silly me! Let's have a peep at him, then . . . There he is, my son, sleeping like a baby . . . and *that* was a pretty daft thing to say, HAW, HAW, HAW!'

Alice crept back to bed. Her sleepwalking, and the nice hot drink she was supposed to have had, seemed to have been forgotten.

Her body lay still, but the thoughts inside her head were shooting off in all directions. What was going to happen now? What could she do, what could she do?

Anyway, her parents didn't suspect, they didn't have the faintest idea what was really going on, and that was one comfort. But Harry didn't have his blanket yet. And there were the feeding bottles that still had to be returned. And the dirty nappy to be disposed of, and she would need more nappies soon . . .

It was impossible. The whole thing was impossible, she would have to give it up.

But I can't give it up, I can't, she thought. I can't give you up, Harry, not now I've found you.

If only I had more *time*.

Just half an hour in the house by myself would do it. I could do a lot in half an hour . . .

Mum will be going out in the morning. Mum will be taking William to the clinic in the morning . . .

Is there some way that *I* could be at home, while Mum is at the clinic . . . ?

There was one way she could try, of course . . .

'Come on, lazybones!' That was Mum, calling Alice to get out of bed.

'I don't feel very well . . . I'm sorry.'

Mum came into the room. 'What's the matter?'

'I feel sick. I think I'm going to be sick.'

Mum regarded her, cheerfully. 'Oh, come on now, you haven't lost your colour . . . I know what it is, you got yourself a bit upset about last night. Up you get, have some breakfast and forget all about it.'

'Can't I just stay home from school?'

'Not in the house by yourself you can't.'

'Oh.'

'Look, you know I have to take William to the clinic. Honestly, I don't think there's anything the matter with you. You'll be fine once you get to school, you'll see!'

Alice washed and dressed herself slowly, trying to think. Downstairs in the kitchen, Mum was feeding William. Dad had gone to work, of course. Dad always left the house early to avoid the rush hour. 'Get yourself some cornflakes,' said Mum. She seemed to have forgotten about Alice's feeling sick.

Alice poured out the cornflakes and milk. She took two swallows, then rushed upstairs to the

39

bathroom. She couldn't force herself to be sick really, but she knew how to make it sound like that.

Downstairs again, dragging her steps. 'Ho, hum,' said Mum. 'Looks like you really *are* a bit poorly. Do you want to go back to bed?'

'Can't I just lie down on the sofa?'

Mum went on with changing William. 'Oh look, another smile! What was that you said, Alice?'

'Can I just lie down on the sofa? Instead of going back to bed?'

'If you like.'

'I'm sorry to be a nuisance. You can still take William to the clinic. I don't mind if you leave me on my own.'

'That's not the point . . . I know you're eleven, but I think it might still be against the law. To leave you in the house on your own, I mean.'

'Oh . . . I'm sorry. I didn't know.'

'All right, I know what, I'll ask Margaret to come in and keep an eye on you. She won't mind for an hour or so.'

Margaret was Mum's friend, sort of, from next door. Margaret was nice, but it was not good news that she was going to be asked to keep an eye on Alice. Alice lay on the sofa and fretted, the turmoil of her thoughts hidden behind the still mouth and expressionless eyes.

At half past eight Miranda called, and Alice heard her being turned away.

Seething with disappointment and frustration, Miranda made her way to school alone. Yesterday evening her rabbits and her ballet class had almost

40

crowded out thoughts of the baby; today the baby was the most exciting thing again.

How was Alice getting along with looking after it? Miranda couldn't wait to find out. It was really too bad of Alice to go and be sick, this morning of all mornings! And was she really sick, or had something happened about the baby in the night? Like, for instance, had her mum found out?

No, it couldn't be that. Alice's mum would have been upset if it was that, not all smiles and easygoing, saying that Alice wasn't coming to school today, but she'd probably be better by tomorrow. Also there would surely have been questions and accusations, and threats to tell Miranda's parents about her part in it all . . . For the first time, Miranda began to feel some twinges of discomfort about that possibility.

But anyway, it hadn't happened, at least not yet, so why worry?

The thing was, there was a whole day to be got through, before she could hold the dear darling sweet little baby again . . . all clean and sweet-smelling now for certain, because Alice was sure to have washed it.

And no one to talk to about it, no one to go into a huddle with in the playground, and whisper to in class.

She could hardly go into any huddles with Edward, people would get the wrong idea. As though she could possibly fancy that silly rude twit! All knobbly and bony, with that sharp hollow face! Ugh!

*

41

Edward made his way through the park. He passed the seat where he found the baby yesterday, and felt a little thrill of excitement all over again. The thrill started in his feet, and prickled its way delightfully the length of his body and through to his scalp, where it quivered and tingled in the roots of his hair.

The thrill was so pleasant that Edward lingered a moment by the seat, enjoying the memory, and going over his plans. He even bent down to examine the space underneath just in case there might, by some chance, be another baby there this morning.

Actually, it might be a good idea to keep a general look-out for babies that had been thrown away. He could always dump them on Alice Cousins, while he scouted around to find buyers for them. He made several detours from the path, poking about in bushes and under seats. He even looked in one or two rubbish bins, because he knew from the television that rubbish bins were favourite for finding abandoned babies.

No luck this morning, though. Edward arrived at school, just as everyone was going inside.

Emily sat slumped on the grass beside the path, because her legs had suddenly become too weak to hold her up. She felt swimmy and faint, and there was a roaring in her ears.

She didn't dare to look.

Was her baby still there, under the seat?

If her baby was still there he might not have lived through the night!

What wicked thing had she done, what had she done?

She must go and see. She must force her trembling legs to take her as far as the seat, and then she would know for certain.

When Emily stood, the world tipped and tilted around her. She was so giddy that for a few moments she had to hold tight to a tree to stop herself from falling down again. Then she stumbled towards the seat, desperate to know and dreading to know.

Nothing!

Her baby had been found, he was somewhere safe, she could relax, and breathe again. That boy, for instance, the one she saw yesterday – perhaps *he* found her baby. Perhaps he took it home to his mum, and his mum looked after it in her house. And washed it and fed it and loved it. Perhaps, right at this minute, Emily's baby was warm and safe, in that boy's house. Anyway she didn't have to worry about being wicked, she didn't have to worry about being a murderer; for a minute or two her heart was almost light.

She would forget all about it, now. She would forget she ever had a baby, and get on with the rest of her life.

Miranda stood in the playground alone, feeling rather lost, as well as frustrated. Usually she and Alice just stayed together at playtimes, didn't bother with the various groups. Concentrating on one best friend was Miranda's style. Not that Alice would have been Miranda's first choice of best friend. Her first choice would have been Rebecca –

43

but when Miranda joined the school, Rebecca already had a best friend, as had most of the other girls. Alice, luckily, had been one of a threesome with Patsy and Claire, who hadn't minded being left as a twosome. So Alice was available, and Alice was good enough, especially as she didn't seem to mind being bossed about.

Only this m'orning, of all mornings, Alice was not there!

Miranda considered tagging herself on to Patsy and Claire for the day, but decided they were too boring. Kind and gentle, but definitely boring. Miranda wandered over to Rebecca and Leanne. 'Want to know something interesting?' She didn't know anything interesting really. Nothing that could be told, that is. She would have to make something up. 'It's about Edward Lawson.'

'What about him?'

'He likes playing with dolls.'

'*What?*' Rebecca laughed her harsh, strident laugh. She was a big girl, good-looking in a flashy way, with a lot of thick dark hair and very white teeth.

'True, I swear it! He played dolls with me and Alice yesterday afternoon after school. In Alice's playhouse.' She shouldn't have picked on a story like that, of course. It was going too dangerously close to the great secret, but she couldn't back out now.

'You're joking!'

'Come on, tell us more!'

'Hey, Flora, Lucy, come and listen to this!'

In class, the word went round. Soon the boys were sniggering as well. Miss Churchwood laughed

44

herself, braying good-naturedly. 'Come on, now, if there's a joke let's all share it.'

Miss Churchwood was not beautiful. She had a long body and short legs, and a silly sort of face with no chin to it. No one knew how much Miss Churchwood minded her silly face, but in her secret heart she was wistfully envious of people like Miranda and Rebecca. What had they done, to deserve their good looks? Not much, as far as Miss Churchwood could see.

Miss Churchwood did not greatly care for Miranda and Rebecca. Indeed, this was not a particularly nice class – Miss Churchwood had known better. She liked Alice, though, she liked her very much indeed. Miss Churchwood thought there was probably a lot more to Alice Cousins than met the eye. Her stories, for instance, showed glimpses of quite a strong imagination, and depths of feeling you wouldn't guess from the stodgy look of her. And she was so helpful!

Miss Churchwood was an enthusiastic teacher, but her enthusiasm did tend to carry her away, sometimes. She forgot where she had put things; Alice always knew where they were. If there was something to be done, at a certain time, Alice would be at her teacher's elbow, right on the moment, shyly and discreetly reminding her. And of course she could be trusted absolutely to carry a message, word for word without getting it wrong.

Miss Churchwood was going to miss Alice, who for some reason was away today.

The class was still restless with half-suppressed mirth. Rebecca spoke up. 'Edward Lawson plays with dolls.'

Edward Lawson! An odd child, a loner, but happy enough in his own little world, as far as Miss Churchwood could tell. She spoke firmly. 'Well, what's wrong with that?'

'He's a *boy*!'

'There's no law that says girls have to like one thing, and boys have to like another,' said Miss Churchwood. 'If Edward is practising to be a good father one day, then good luck to him, say I!'

Edward, who had been too angry to speak, found his voice. 'It's not true, though, she made it up!'

'No, I didn't.'

'Well, Miranda did, then.'

This was the sort of argument that could go on for ever; Miss Churchwood decided it was time to put the lid on. 'Come on now, everyone. There are only so many hours in the day, and this one is for working on our topic folders. Don't you agree, Rebecca?'

If Rebecca agreed, hopefully everyone else would also. Rebecca shrugged, and bent over her table. The class settled, all except Edward who was too upset to concentrate on his work. It was worrying enough Alice Cousins being away today, without having to deal with all this rubbish, he thought furiously. He would have to get on with selling his baby quickly, before anything went really wrong.

But at playtime, he found himself cornered by a group of taunting girls. Hateful females, not a brain between them, getting in his way so he couldn't begin his enquiries. Frantically, he tried to make his escape.

The girls formed a ring around him, making a game out of it. Every time Edward lunged at a space in the ring, one of the girls stepped neatly in front of him, barring his escape. And the time was going by! This precious playtime, so short, so soon to be over, and he had made no progress at all in finding a buyer for his baby. 'If you don't get out of my way I'm going to hit somebody, I mean it!' He wasn't frightened of them of course, not really. The tears he found in his eyes were tears of rage, not fear, of course they were.

'Oh, let the cry-baby go!' Rebecca jeered.

Edward took refuge in the boys' toilets. There were a few younger boys inside, but none he knew very well, and you could hardly walk up to a Year Four boy whose name you couldn't even remember and start a casual conversation about how sad it was that some people wanted babies and didn't have them.

He ventured outside, and was immediately surrounded by a small crowd who wanted to buy apples and crisps. 'I haven't got any. Not today.'

'But you said!'

'I changed my mind. I didn't have time, all right?'

'But you *said*! I brought my money – look!'

'Oh, get lost!' Out of the corner of his eye, Edward had spotted Keith, from his class, meandering towards the toilets. Keith had a large family – millions of aunts and uncles and grown-up cousins. Surely one of Keith's millions of relations would be in the market for a cheap baby! Edward fell into step beside him. 'I was watching the telly last night,' he offered, conversationally.

47

Keith grunted.

'It was a good programme – all about people that want babies, and can't have them.'

Keith blinked at him, from behind thick glasses. 'What do you mean?'

Edward swallowed his impatience. Not only half blind, half witted as well! '*You* know! People that try to have babies, but there's something wrong with them, so the babies don't come.'

'Oh.'

'Did you ever meet anybody like that?'

' . . . Yeah.'

'You *did*?'

' . . . Yeah.'

The whistle shrilled across the playground.

4

Discovered!

Mum had taken William to the clinic, and Margaret from next door had come in to keep an eye on Alice.

Margaret was one of those big, untidy women you can't help liking. Her clothes rarely matched each other very well – today's blouse, for instance, was all pink and yellow roses, while her trousers were a mass of orange and purple squiggles. Her hair was done up in a sort of bun, from which strands were continually escaping, to hang like wilting grass round her apple-red cheeks. She looked a mess, but she smelled like fresh air, and her smile was like sunshine, always.

'Well, well, what have you been doing to yourself? Eaten something didn't agree with you?' Margaret's voice rang out clear, and musical, and warm.

'Actually, I'm feeling a bit better now,' said Alice.

'Something to eat, then? Or drink?'

Alice was starving, having had only one mouthful of breakfast, but thought it might be unwise to be *too* much better, too soon. 'I thought perhaps I could go in the garden, and lie under the tree, on the lawn. Get some fresh air.'

Margaret considered. 'Well – that's not a bad idea.'

'On Mum's sun-lounger.'

'Why not? I'll get it out for you, shall I?'

'Yes please. If it's not too much trouble.'

Alice lay in the shade, the scent of new-mown grass still strong in her nostrils, and wondered how to manage the next bit. 'You don't have to stay with me really. I'm sure you've got lots of things to do . . . Like in your garden, haven't you got things you want to do in your garden?'

Margaret's garden was her pride and joy. She laughed. 'Oh, that! That's never-ending!'

'Well, why don't you go and do some of it? You can keep an eye on me through the fence.'

'True . . . Are you sure?'

'I don't want to be a nuisance.'

'*Alice*! When have you ever been a nuisance in your life?' She's a nice child, Margaret thought. I wish she was mine! 'That was a kind thought of yours, and do you know, I think I'll take you up on it. I'll just pop round and get my gloves, and my tools. Five minutes, and then you'll see me in my garden!'

Five minutes, Alice thought. Five minutes ought to be long enough to make another feed for Harry. Not to give it him, though. And he must be getting hungry again; it's a wonder he hasn't cried, and somebody heard! She strained her ears, anxiously, as she watched Margaret's broad behind disappearing round the side of the house.

Then she ran.

By the time Margaret reappeared, in her own garden, the feed was all ready, wrapped in yet another towel to keep it warm, and safely hidden under the sun-lounger. Margaret waved, and Alice waved back. Then most of Margaret disappeared from sight; only her large behind could be seen, bending over behind some shrubs. She would look up now and again, Alice supposed, but hopefully not too soon.

Alice ran, again.

Bending over Harry, Alice thought her heart would burst with love. His little face, surely sweeter than yesterday, was relaxed and trusting in sleep. She touched him gently; his cheek was warm – he hadn't missed his blanket too much.

It was a pity to wake him, but he would need changing, Alice thought, as well as feeding, and she had to take her chance while it was there. Now there were two used nappies as well as the three used bottles to be dealt with. And more things to be fetched from the house. Baby wipes she had, and one more nappy left. Harry should have another bath really, but that was too difficult to organise. She looked for something to wrap the nappies in, and wished she had thought of bringing a plastic bag from the house. There was the towel he had come in, of course. Alice felt guilty about throwing away a perfectly good towel, but there was nothing for it . . .

Margaret was looking through the fence and smiling. 'Oh, *there* you are! I was wondering where you'd got to.'

She didn't ask what was in the pink and white bundle, perhaps because she was too polite, or perhaps because she didn't think it was important; it was hard to tell which. At any rate Alice thought it might look rather peculiar if she just sat down with the bundle in her lap, so she took it straight to the bin which stood next to the new garden shed. She thrust it deep down, so it was covered with potato peelings and banana skins. Then she decided to push her luck still further. 'I'm just going to the loo,' she announced.

'You're not feeling sick again, are you?'

'No, no, I just want to – you know . . .'

'Oh, right!'

She would get the nappies – a whole packet of them this time. Of course Mum might notice if a whole packet disappeared, but she'd just have to chance it. And what about a jar of cream for Harry's bottom? There was only one jar that she could see – dared she take it? No, no, that was going too far! What else, then? Oh yes – a nice clean blanket. The ones in the pram had gone to the clinic with William, but there were more in the airing cupboard. Alice took two.

Now – how to get them to the playhouse? She could hide the things in a large plastic bag, if she could find one, but it would still look funny to be going up and down the garden too often when she was supposed to be ill . . . Supposing she were to leave the bundle in the conservatory, until Margaret went into her house or something . . . ?

Alice's tummy rumbled emptily as she plodded down the stairs, but she was past being hungry now. She had forgotten the clothes, she realised, but that would have to wait. In the kitchen she found the large plastic bag she was looking for.

Margaret waved again, as Alice passed on her way to the sun-lounger. 'All right?'

'Yes thank you.'

Margaret smiled her sunshiny smile. 'You're so

much better you'll be going to school this afternoon, I shouldn't wonder!'

Oh dear, oh no, that wouldn't do! She must stay home, she must! She must stay close to Harry. Her baby, her baby – she couldn't bear to be more than a few metres away from him. No, no, she must stay home all day!

And tomorrow?

And the next two days?

The day after that would be Saturday, when she would be home anyway. But what about next week?

Perhaps she could be ill for a week. For two weeks! It wouldn't matter if she didn't have anything to eat for two weeks, it could even be a good thing! If she didn't eat anything for two weeks she would get nice and thin, wouldn't she? As thin as Miranda perhaps, or Mum!

Alice shook her head slowly, at Margaret. 'Actually, I didn't like to say but actually, actually I was sick again, when I went to the bathroom . . . I'm sorry.' She was *deeply* sorry about having to tell lies to Margaret, but it was all for Harry's sake, wasn't it?

'Oh, you poor kid!'

'I'm sorry.'

'Don't be silly. Look, can't I get you anything? A drink of water or something?'

'All right. A drink of water would be nice.'

'Just a tick. You go and lie down again. I'll be right round, OK?'

As soon as Margaret was out of sight, Alice ran. She dumped her parcel in the playhouse, and scurried back to the sun-lounger. Not used to all this hurrying she was still breathing rather heavily when Margaret appeared once more. Margaret looked concerned. 'I wonder if you've got a temperature.' She put a large hand on Alice's forehead. 'Do you know, I believe you have; you're sweating! Now you just have a sip of this water, and then lie down and rest till your mum comes home.'

She would have to do that, Alice thought. Now she had said about being sick, she couldn't suddenly change her story again. And Margaret would *really* be watching now . . .

But how to get into the playhouse . . . ?

Had she made a mistake saying that about feeling worse?

I'm all in a muddle, she thought, fighting panic. And I haven't got anybody to help me sort it out . . .

At lunch time, Miranda and Rebecca sat with their heads close together, whispering and giggling. Leanne, clearly jealous, kept trying to butt in – her sharp-featured face growing pink from the effort, her eyes, small and close together, sparking resentment. But Rebecca was paying more and more attention to Miranda, who was getting more and more excited by this success. What were her chances, Miranda wondered, of enticing Rebecca away from Leanne for good?

Leanne wandered away, in a huff, to join another group. Giddy with recklessness, Miranda cupped her hand over Rebecca's ear and whispered: 'Do you want to know a secret? A really exciting secret? A really, really *really* exciting secret that you would never guess in the world what it is?'

'Come on, then, what?'

'Swear you won't tell anyone!'

'OK.'

'No, swear; you have to swear properly, all right?'

'I hope I drop dead if I tell – is that good enough?'

'No, you have to say *I hope I drop dead and go to the Bad Place.*'

Rebecca was willing to consign herself to the Bad Place.

Miranda took a deep breath . . .

Edward manoeuvred Keith into a corner of the playground. 'You know what you said this morning?'

'What about?'

'*You* know! About people that can't have babies. You said you know somebody like that.'

'Oh, yeah . . .'

'I think it's sad. Don't you think it's sad?'

'My aunty's going to have an operation though. To help her make one.'

Edward struggled to conceal his delight. 'What, in hospital?'

'I think so . . . Yeah, in hospital.'

'Will it hurt?'

'I dunno. I suppose so.'

Edward whistled through his teeth. 'All that trouble? Why doesn't she just buy one? One that's already made?'

'I dunno.'

'Hasn't she got any money?'

'*I* dunno.'

'Where does your aunty live?'

'Next door to me . . .' Keith was suddenly suspicious. 'What do you want to know for?'

Edward laughed a carefully casual laugh. 'Only joking . . . Just being nosy.'

Mum came back from the clinic radiating pleasure and satisfaction. William was doing fine. He was putting on just the right amount of weight, and all his workings were in excellent order. He was also, in Mum's opinion, quite the most beautiful baby on display that day. Furthermore, someone she got talking to had refused to believe that William's mother was old enough to be also the mother of an eleven-year-old daughter! She looked young and pretty, she reflected with satisfaction, and she had a beautiful baby – what more could any woman want?

Then she remembered about Alice.

Margaret confided her concerns out of earshot of the 'invalid' still lying on the sun-lounger in the shade.

'She's been sick again, you know. And she seems to have a temperature. I'm wondering if she might be coming down with something.'

'Ho, hum . . . I suppose I shall have to take her to the doctor after all . . . Did she tell you about the sleepwalking?'

'No. When was this?'

'Last night. Downstairs in her nighty, and didn't seem to know how she got there.'

'Has she got something on her mind, do you suppose? Something bothering her?'

'*Alice*?' Alice's mother dismissed that idea with a

laugh. 'I don't think anything ever troubles Alice much.'

Margaret wondered about that. 'Anyway, she's clearly not well.'

Alice's mother frowned. 'I was hoping she'd be all right for school this afternoon. You couldn't . . . ?' She put her head on one side and gave Margaret her most beguiling smile. 'I suppose you couldn't be an absolute angel and mind her for another hour or so while I go to Sainsbury's?'

'Now?'

'About two-thirty? I know you have to get Bill his lunch – how *is* Bill, by the way?'

Margaret shook her head, and the sunshiny smile faded. 'Not good. Won't get out of his chair. Won't even watch television. Just sits there, brooding.'

'All over not having a job?'

'It's made him feel he's not worth anything . . . I daren't even *suggest* that *I* should get one . . . At least we don't have money worries, as long as we're careful.'

'About two-thirty, then? For minding Alice?'

'I'll have William as well, if you like.'

'Oh, you *are* an absolute angel!'

Rebecca whispered to Leanne. '*I* know a secret. Something you'd never guess. Something you'd never guess in a million years.'

'What is it?'

'You have to swear not to tell anyone.'

'All right, I swear.'

'You have to swear properly.'

'OK, I swear I hope to die if I tell.'

57

'Not good enough. You have to swear you hope to die and go to the Bad Place, if you tell anyone at all in the world. I mean it, Leanne!'

Leanne, who didn't actually believe in the Bad Place, judged it advantageous to pretend that she did.

Rebecca took a deep breath . . .

William's pram was on Margaret's lawn, and Alice was still lying on the sun-lounger, where Margaret could keep an eye on her through the fence, as before. She had waited for this moment, longed for it, and now that it had come she was still very unclear about how best to use it.

Make another feed for Harry first, she thought. That was not difficult. Margaret would not question her need to go into the house, and it wouldn't much matter how long she was there, since being 'sick' again could take ages and ages if she wanted it to.

The problem was being seen to go to the playhouse, when she was supposed to be so ill.

She managed to conceal the new feed under her dress, as she walked slowly back to the sun-lounger. 'All right?' Margaret called to her.

Alice was about to say that, unfortunately, she *had* been sick yet again, when an idea suddenly struck her. It was too late for her to go to school now! She could quite safely make a recovery now! 'Yes thank you,' she called. 'I'm feeling a lot better actually . . . I think I'll go down to the playhouse and get something to do . . . Like a book to read, perhaps.'

Margaret beamed. 'Oh, you do that! I *am* glad you're feeling so much better.'

Alice made herself *walk* to the playhouse. She mustn't be too much better, she mustn't be seen to be running, even though she couldn't wait to get to him. Her baby! She held him in her arms, rocking him, cuddling him, loving him. She changed his nappy, but he didn't seem to want his feed. She wrapped the bottle in one of William's blankets, and hoped it would keep warm enough for later.

Alice could have sat there all day, just holding her baby and being happy, but there were things to be done – one thing in particular that couldn't be safely left any longer. She wasn't sure how many spare feeding bottles Mum had for William, but it was sure to be noticed this evening if *four* were missing. She must get three of them to the kitchen, and washed and sterilised. She knew how to do it; she had helped Mum with that chore often enough. The problem was time. And an excuse to go back to the house again.

Should she have another relapse?

No, no, there was a better idea. She couldn't find an interesting book in the playhouse, she would say – she must go to her bedroom to look there. And that could take ages, and ages, and ages, if need be . . .

The washing and sterilising safely accomplished, Alice emerged from the house with her book, and went to lie down on the sun-lounger once more, but Margaret called to her over the fence. 'Alice! Have you got a cat?'

'No . . . We used to . . . You know, Zebedee. But he died.'

Margaret was looking puzzled. 'I know Zebedee died. I thought perhaps you might have got a new one. A kitten.'

'No . . . Mum said it wasn't worth the trouble to have another one.'

'It's just I heard something, when I went to the bottom of the garden. Almost like a baby crying.'

Alice's heart began to hammer, and she felt suddenly faint. '*I* can't hear anything,' she managed to say.

'Well I can't, here . . . It was when I went down the bottom to see to—'

'Perhaps it's in the garden behind.'

'Perhaps . . .'

There was a sudden wail from the pram on Margaret's lawn. Oh thank you, William! Thank you, Alice thought. You woke up just in time. Margaret crossed over and picked William out of his pram, holding him lovingly against her shoulder, patting and rubbing his back to soothe him.

'I expect that's what you heard before,' said Alice, hopefully.

Margaret walked William up and down, murmuring endearing words into his ear, until he stopped crying. Alice stood by the fence, making herself talk in a louder voice than usual, to keep Margaret's attention. 'Did *you* ever have a baby, Margaret?'

'No.'

'Didn't you want to have one?'

'Very much. I just wasn't lucky.' Margaret put

William back in his pram. She straightened up, and looked like making for the bottom of her garden again.

'Couldn't you adopt one?'

'They say I'm too old,' said Margaret, simply.

'Oh . . . Aren't you going to go on weeding here? And talking to me?'

'I will in a minute – there's just something I want to—'

Three-quarters of the way down the path, Margaret put her head on one side, clearly listening. 'Do you know,' she called, 'I think it's coming from your playhouse, Alice! That sound I mentioned before . . . I'm *sure* it's coming from your playhouse!'

Alice tried desperately hard to be sick right where she was, but could only manage some strained dry retching sounds. Margaret stood watching her, a thoughtful expression on her face. Then she walked slowly back. 'Alice, I think there might be a kitten or something, trapped in your playhouse.'

'There isn't, there isn't!'

'Well, now, do you know, I think we should go and look together . . . In case something alive has got in there by mistake.'

'There's nothing there!'

'Perhaps not. But I think we should go and find out for sure, don't you?'

Alice stood looking her most wooden.

'Perhaps you wanted a kitten, only your mum wouldn't let you have one, so you thought you'd have it all by yourself, is that it?'

Alice went on looking wooden.

61

'Look – it's better if we sort it out together, than if we wait till your mum comes home, don't you think? Perhaps we can find a way round it, even.'

Two large tears welled up in the corner of Alice's eyes, and rolled slowly down her cheeks. Margaret was deeply concerned; she had never known Alice cry, ever. She didn't smile all that often either, or laugh – but cry, *never*. 'Come on, now,' Margaret coaxed. 'Don't upset yourself.'

Suddenly it was not just silent weeping, it was a storm of wild, hysterical grief. Alice doubled up, sobbing uncontrollably, catching at her breath, choking. Margaret regarded the sight in dismay for a moment, then moved as fast as her bulk would allow. She grabbed at William's pram and steered it full tilt around the side of her own house and into the Cousins' back garden.

Alice could not be seen, but she could be heard even at this distance. Margaret left William's pram outside the conservatory, and made for where the sobbing was.

Inside the playhouse Alice stood, clutching something to her chest. Something wrapped in a blanket. Something whose own thin wails were being almost drowned out by Alice's desolate, desperate, crying. Margaret stared in disbelief. 'Dear God!' she exclaimed. 'It *is* a baby!'

Alice heaved a great gulp and found her speech. 'He's mine! You can't take him away, he's mine!'

'All right, all right . . . It's all right, Alice . . .'

'It's not all right, you're going to take him away. And you can't. He's mine.'

'Look . . . I mean . . .' Margaret found herself helplessly lost for words. Well, what *is* a person supposed to say in a situation like this? 'Look, dear,' she spoke as gently as she knew how, 'Alice dear, you must know you're not old enough to look after a baby, all by yourself.'

'But he's mine! His mum didn't want him, she threw him away. So now he's mine. And you can't take him away, nobody can, I'm not going to let them!'

The sobbing began again. 'Hush!' said Margaret. The sobbing grew louder. All sorts of thoughts were shooting through Margaret's head – crazy thoughts, impossible thoughts . . .

Impossible . . . ?

Totally impossible . . . ?

'Alice, does anybody else know about this? Anybody except you?'

The sobbing grew louder still. Margaret closed the space between them and put her arms round Alice and the baby together. She rocked them, and soothed them, passing her hand up and down Alice's back as she had so recently done for William. 'Alice, hush! Listen! No, listen, listen to me . . .'

There was no doubt about it, Margaret thought, what she was about to say was probably mad. She was taking leave of her senses, she must be! And yet here was this chance . . . It might even be *meant* . . . Miracles did happen sometimes . . .

Margaret took a deep breath and heard herself voicing the unbelievable: 'Listen, Alice . . . If nobody knows about this except you, there might be a way for you to keep the baby.'

Alice stepped back, out of the circle of Margaret's arms, staring round-eyed. '*What*!'

'It would have to be a secret, though. A secret between you and me. Can you keep a secret?'

'. . . Yes.'

'He can't stay here, of course. You will have to let me take him to my house.'

'But he'll still be my baby?'

'Yes, he'll still be your baby. And you can come and see him every day. And bath him. And feed him, and cuddle him . . . Would you like that?'

Would she *like* it! All the joy in the world was shining in her face now.

'And Mum and Dad wouldn't know?'

'*Nobody* will know. Unless you tell them . . . Alice, there *isn't* anyone who knows about this already, is there, except you?'

Alice swallowed. If it was so important for no one else to know, then she must say no one else knew. 'Only me,' she lied.

'Because if the police find out we kept him, instead of handing him over, we'll be in big trouble.'

'Me as well?'

'Yes, you as well,' said Margaret firmly. 'I don't want to frighten you, but it's terribly important you understand. If the police find out they'll take the baby away, *and* we'll both be in big trouble.'

'Do you mean I might go to prison?'

'Well – you might!' Margaret was immediately sorry she'd said anything so drastic, and so untrue, so she tried to soften it a bit. 'Well, perhaps not that, but like I said, there'd be big trouble, and the police would certainly be involved.'

'Oh.'

'I suppose you found him . . . Where did you

find the baby, Alice? All right, all right, tell me another time . . . We have to be quick now, before your mum gets back.' Margaret glanced swiftly around the little playhouse, gathering up feeding bottle, used nappy, tea towels and blankets – anything that might betray the recent presence of a young baby. 'Come on,' she said to Alice. 'We'll put them all in William's pram, and get them round to my house pronto . . . And the baby, of course.'

'His name is Harry,' said Alice.

'Well now,' said Margaret. 'That's a lovely name.'

'And I found him in the park. In a paper bag. Under a seat.'

'I see.'

5

Baby for sale

Miranda ran joyfully around the side of Alice's house. The moment had come at last. At last she was going to hold the darling, sweet, lovely little baby in her arms again. Her heart danced with excitement.

Alice's mother lay on the sun-lounger, with William's pram beside her. Alice sprawled on the grass, a little way off. Alice's mother opened one lazy eye, and jerked her head in Alice's direction. 'She's better,' she informed Miranda. 'As you can see.'

'Mum was going to take me to the doctor, but she's not now.' For some reason, Alice seemed unwilling to meet Miranda's eyes.

There was a tiresome little shadow of apprehension, which Miranda brushed impatiently aside. 'Shall we go to the playhouse, then?' She hopped from leg to leg, radiating eagerness.

Alice rose slowly to her feet.

Miranda led the way, and Alice plodded behind. Inside the playhouse, Miranda gazed in puzzlement. 'Where is he? Where have you put him?'

'He's gone.'

'What do you mean, gone? Gone where?'

'I don't know. He's just gone. I'm sorry.'

Miranda searched Alice's face, but Alice's

expression was giving nothing away. 'I don't understand. What happened?'

'Somebody must have stolen him. I came down in the night, but he wasn't there. That's all I know.' She hated lying to Miranda, but what else could she do? Margaret said no one else must know. And of course Miranda *did* know, some of it, and Edward too. The best Alice could do was to keep the rest of it a secret.

Miranda was outraged at Alice's news. 'We have to tell the police!'

Alice's heart began to pound. 'No, no – we can't!'

'Why not?'

'Because we'll have to explain how we had him in the first place. And we'll get in trouble for it. Big trouble. *Very* big trouble . . . We might even have to go to prison!'

'Oh . . . I didn't think of that.'

'Neither I didn't think of it either. Only after he got stolen I started to think of it. We shall have to keep it all a secret for ever and ever. You will have to promise, Miranda!'

'Well, of course. *I* don't want to go to prison . . . What about Edward, though?'

'We shall have to tell Edward to keep it a secret as well.'

Miranda's face had clouded over, but now it suddenly brightened. 'Edward is going to be very cross,' she said with satisfaction.

'I know.'

'Actually, I can't wait to see how cross horrible Edward is going to be!'

'All I'm worried about,' said Alice, 'is if he keeps the secret.'

'Well, he'll have to, won't he?' Miranda assured her. 'He won't want to go to prison, nobody would.' A nasty thought suddenly struck her. *Rebecca.* What a pity she already told Rebecca. Oh, but Rebecca had promised! Forget Rebecca. Forget the whole thing. 'Let's not think any more about the baby now. The baby is finished, OK? I think I had enough of the baby anyway. You tell Edward I can't be bothered. Now let's play something else!'

Alice felt a sudden rush of something like pure happiness. Everything was coming right, like a miracle! She had been whisked out of trouble, she still had her baby, and she still had Miranda for her best friend.

Any more joy than this would be more than she could bear; it would be too much!

Edward was tailing Keith home. This was great fun, especially as there was Keith's younger brother to keep hiding from, as well as Keith himself. From time to time Keith and his brother stopped to dawdle, or scribble with chalk on someone's wall, or engage in a little punch-up between themselves; and every time that happened, Edward had to nip into someone's drive, or crouch behind someone's hedge, so that he wouldn't be seen.

Keith himself, of course, was of no interest whatsoever, and neither was his brother. The interesting person was Keith's aunty, who wanted a baby and couldn't have one unless she went to hospital for an operation. Little did she suspect the wonderful news that she was soon to hear. Little did she know the joy that Edward was about to bring her!

Ah! Keith and his brother had turned into a house at last! Now the question was, the big question *was* – which of Keith's two next doors did his aunty live at?

Edward rang the bell at the first one. There was no answer, so he tried the knocker as well. At last, at long last, the door opened. Not fully – there was a chain connecting the door with the door frame, leaving a narrow crack, through which could just be seen the face of an ancient crone; someone who must be a hundred years old, at least. There was a whiff of sourness, and staleness, as though the windows of this house were never opened.

Edward knew very little about these things, but it did seem to him rather unlikely that the person behind the door would be the person who was going to hospital for an operation to make her have a baby. Nevertheless, it was important to make sure. 'Are you Keith's aunty?' he asked.

'WHAT?' The old lady shouted her question so loud that Edward stepped back, cupping his ears with his hands to protect the drums.

'Keith's aunty?' he said again.

'SPEAK UP! I CAN'T HEAR YOU!'

'KEITH'S AUNTY!' Edward bellowed in return.

'I DON'T KNOW ANYTHING ABOUT ANYTHING.'

'KEITH'S AUNTY?' Edward tried again, but without much hope.

'GO AWAY AND DON'T BOTHER ME. PEOPLE ARE ALWAYS BOTHERING ME. I

DON'T KNOW ANYTHING ABOUT ANY-
THING!'

The door was banged in Edward's face; which
made it safe to conclude, Edward reasoned, that
this was definitely not the person he had been
seeking.

He bent low as he passed the next house,
keeping close to the hedge in case Keith or his
brother might be looking out of a window. The
one after must be it! Edward's heart began to beat
with just a little nervousness. He rang the bell.

This time a man answered. 'Well?' The man's
clothes and face were streaked with white, and
there was a strong smell of fresh paint.

'Are you Keith's uncle?'

'Keith lives next door. I don't know if he's back
from school yet.'

'It's not Keith I want to see. Actually, it's his
aunty.'

'What do you mean?'

'The person I want to see is Keith's aunty.'

'What about?'

'It's private.'

'Well, it won't be private from me. Whatever it
is.'

'I'd rather say it to her, though. You're not the
one that's going to have the operation, are you?'

'*Operation*? What are you talking about?'

'Well, actually I've come to tell her she doesn't
have to have the operation after all . . . Only the
police mustn't know, because it might be against
the law . . . Anyway, I think so; I'm not really sure.'

The man stared. 'What loony bin have you
escaped from, then?'

'None. You don't understand . . . All right, I'll tell you. I've got something to sell.' Edward winked, contorting his face several times. 'I can't say it any clearer here because it might be against the law, but if you would let me come inside, we can settle on a price.'

'I haven't a clue what you're talking about, but we don't want to buy anything, and we are rather busy just now, so would you just like to push off?'

'You're missing a big opportunity.'

'And *you*'re not listening to me. I said *push off*!'

Once more, the door was slammed in Edward's face.

Leanne, Flora and Lucy were being driven home by Leanne's mother, whose turn it was to do the school run that day. The girls sat together in the back seat, left alone for a few minutes while Leanne's mother popped into the jeweller's to see about getting her watch battery changed. 'This is boring,' Flora complained.

Leanne struggled with herself. After all, she had promised. But the excitement in her chest had a life of its own. It swelled, and grew, until it was too big to be kept inside any more. '*I* know something not boring,' she said.

'Bet you don't!'

'Bet I do, then – but you have to promise not to tell . . .'

In class next morning, there was once again much whispering and giggling. 'Oh come on,' said Miss Churchwood. 'What is it this time?'

More giggling.

71

'Actually, I don't think it's true,' said Flora.

'*What* isn't true?'

'Well, they're saying . . . They're saying that Alice and Miranda have got a real live baby.'

'In Alice's playhouse,' said Lucy.

'That they found,' Flora added.

Deathly silence now, while Miss Churchwood caught her breath. Swallowing his fury, Edward glared at the floor.

Miranda had gone very red. She opened her mouth once or twice, but no words came out. 'Miranda?' said Miss Churchwood.

'. . . It was a joke,' Miranda said at last. 'Alice and I made it up for a joke . . . Didn't we, Alice?'

Speechless with fear and dismay, Alice just managed to nod.

Miss Churchwood sighed. 'Don't you think, Year Six, that you're all getting a bit too big for that kind of joke? So let's just get on with something real, shall we?'

In the playground, however, feelings still ran high. The girls gathered in a group, with Alice hovering on the edge of it, terrified that somehow the truth might still come out. 'Who told you?' Rebecca demanded of Flora and Lucy.

'Leanne.'

Rebecca was furious. 'I hate you, Leanne, you weren't supposed to say anything!'

Miranda could have pointed out that Rebecca hadn't been supposed to say anything, either, but she was more than prepared to forgive Rebecca. The great thing, the thing that was to be encouraged, was this rift that seemed to be opening up between Rebecca and Leanne.

'I shall never tell you a secret again, ever!' Rebecca stormed at her best friend, to Miranda's delight.

'You're just as bad as me. You told!'

Rebecca struggled to defend her position. 'Yes, well I only told one person. You told *two*.'

'. . . It was because of Leanne it got spread round the class,' said Miranda, cunningly.

Now Leanne was getting most of the blame, Rebecca was beginning to feel more comfortable with herself. 'Actually I never really believed it,' she claimed. 'I knew it was only a joke really.'

'It was a good joke, wasn't it?' said Miranda, all smiles. 'Leanne believed it.'

'Leanne can't help it if she's stupid,' Rebecca condescended, linking arms with Miranda. 'Leanne can't help it if she's a stupid babble-mouth, that doesn't know the difference between a joke and the real truth.'

Alice saw the linking of arms and felt a coldness, a sort of shrivelling in her heart, followed by a sense of enormous relief that at least Harry was still safely hers. They believed it, didn't they? They all believed that the story about the baby was a joke! Alice held on to that thought, wrapping herself around it.

After play, Rebecca chose Miranda to be her partner in PE, and Leanne had to have Alice because there was no one else. Leanne glared venom at Alice, and Alice sensed herself shrinking under the force of Leanne's hostility. She had always tried so hard to make people like her – or, if not like her at least not *dis*like her. And it wasn't fair, what was happening now, but she was helpless to stop it.

Worse still, sadder still, was the way she was losing Miranda. Miranda wanted Rebecca now, not her; the thing she had been afraid of for so long was happening at last, and it hurt, dreadfully, but she was helpless to stop that also.

There was no need for Alice to be seen in the playground at lunch time, shamefully all alone with no friends. She could have joined up with Patsy and Claire again, but somehow she was too wretched to make the effort. So she found a corner and tried to melt into it, tried to be invisible so no one would notice her; made herself think about Harry, who after all was more important to her than Miranda or anything else, wasn't he!

Edward found her, in her corner. 'I suppose it was that brain-dead Miranda who blabbed. Silly cow!'

Edward! Alice had forgotten all about Edward, who had to be put in the picture, and made to understand he must never tell!

She began to tremble. 'I have to tell you something.'

'Oh, what's that?' He hoped it wasn't anything tiresome. He had planned to put a few more feelers round the school that morning. Have another go at finding someone who wanted to buy his baby. They couldn't all be as stupid as Keith's stupid uncle!

'The baby's gone. I'm sorry.'

Edward gaped. 'What do you mean, *gone*? Gone where?'

'I don't know. Someone came and stole him in the night . . . I'm sorry.'

'*What*!'

'It wasn't my fault.'

'You were supposed to be looking after him!'

'I know . . . I couldn't help it if someone came and took him though, could I? I couldn't stay in the playhouse all night.'

Edward was silent. His hopes all vanished, his plans all come to nothing. 'There goes my money!' he said, bitterly.

'What do you mean? What money?'

There was no point in pretending any more. 'The money for the baby, of course. The money I was going to sell him for.'

Alice gazed at Edward, unbelieving. '*You were going to sell the baby!*' Her face was certainly showing what she felt at that moment.

'Of course. What was the use of him, otherwise?'

'But you were going to – *sell* him!'

'I was going to give you some of the money. I was going to be fair.'

Alice's face went blank again. 'Well anyway, you can't now because he's gone.'

Edward scowled, his face dark and twisted in thought. 'Who could have taken him, though?'

'Well, I suppose . . . a burglar!'

'Burglars don't come to steal babies, they come to steal tellies, and jewellery, and things like that . . . Anyway, who would know he was there?'

' . . . I suppose they heard him.'

Edward shook his head. 'Right down the bottom of the garden, though? . . . No, somebody must have known . . . I've got it, the people in the house next to you!'

Alice was panic-stricken. '*No!*'

'Well, it must have been . . . somebody who saw. Looking out of the window, when we brought him in. Come on, Alice, think!'

'It couldn't have been Number 23; they both go out to work.'

'All right, then the other side. Who lives the other side?'

'Well . . . Margaret and Bill. But I'm sure—'

'Are they home in the day?'

Pointless to deny it. 'Yes, but I'm sure—'

'It's them!' said Edward in triumph. 'They took him, and that's all right, but they have to pay. It was my baby, so they have to pay.'

He's going to go and ask them, Alice thought in horror. He's going to go and tell them he knows. He's going to tell them he was the one that found the baby, and ask them for money. And I said no one knows, only me. So Margaret will find out I told a lie . . .

What will happen then? Will it still be my baby? And there can be all sorts of trouble besides, perhaps . . .

I don't know, I don't know what to do . . .

In desperation, she grabbed a wild idea out of the air. 'Look, what I told you before, it wasn't true,' she whispered.

'What are you talking about now?'

'The baby's dead. He died.'

'WHAT!'

'I'm sorry. I did try to look after him, but he just died. In the night.' It was a dreadful thing to say; Alice could hardly believe she was hearing herself saying it.

'Oh,' said Edward.

'I'm sorry I told you a lie before.'

'I don't get it. I don't get any of it.'

'It was because of Miranda. It was to be the same as what I told Miranda. I didn't want her to know the baby was dead, I thought she would be too upset.'

'Oh.'

It was a nasty shock – what a thing to happen! Fancy the baby going and dying, poor little thing! Babies did die sometimes, of course – why hadn't he thought of that? Perhaps they should have taken it to the hospital after all ... Alice had wanted to take it to the hospital ... It wasn't a nice thing to think that the baby might have died because he wouldn't let it be taken to the hospital ...

He pushed the thought away.

'So what did you do with the ... you know ... with the ...'

'I buried it. In the garden.'

'Oh.'

'You won't tell anyone, will you?'

'What would I do that for?'

'I don't know. Only I think we could all get in a lot of trouble if you do ... We might even have to go to prison ... Because we kept it when we shouldn't have.'

'Yeah.' Perhaps kids could go to prison after all; perhaps he had been wrong about that. Not for stealing cars, or breaking into houses, he didn't think they could go to prison for that – but for not taking babies to the hospital . . . ? And now the baby had died . . .

'So it's best really if we don't talk about it any more. At all. I think.'

Edward agreed. Best not talk about it any more, best not think about it any more. Best find some other plan for being a millionaire and think about that *hard*. He was amazed, though – amazed at Alice, who had seemed pretty soft, on the whole, and yet had been cool enough, and tough enough, to bury a dead baby in her own back garden!

Miranda and Alice walked home together as usual, but there was an awkwardness between them. 'I liked that story Miss Churchwood read to us, didn't you?' said Miranda.

'Yes,' said Alice, 'it was good.' She wasn't going to fight for Miranda – what was the use? She must just let her go, then it wouldn't hurt so much.

Miranda tried again. 'It is a really hot day today, isn't it?'

'Yes, it is hot.'

At the gate of Alice's house there was more awkwardness. 'I think I better go straight home this afternoon,' said Miranda, uncomfortably.

'All right, then.'

'We're going swimming tonight, and I have to do my homework first.'

'All right, then.'

When Miranda went swimming, with her father or her older brother and sister, Alice often went with them, but this evening she evidently wasn't going to be invited. It did hurt not to be invited . . . But then, there were other things she wanted to do, weren't there? Things Miranda would have got in the way of. Oh, Harry, Harry, Alice's heart cried. I can't wait to hold you, I just can't wait!

'See you tomorrow, then,' she said to Miranda, swallowing the small lump of pain in her throat.

'OK, see you tomorrow.' Miranda danced off with a light heart. Alice was not going to be difficult; she was not going to be jealous, or make a silly fuss. They could still be friends sort of, Miranda thought vaguely. Sometimes. Now and again after school. It just wouldn't do to have boring ordinary Alice clinging on all the time. Not now she had Rebecca!

On the back lawn, Alice's mother was stretched out in the sun as usual. 'Ho, hum, no Miranda?'

'She's busy . . . Is it all right if I go in and see Margaret?'

'Well – I suppose so.'

'She was going to show me something. She said about it yesterday.'

'Go on then – don't be too long!'

Mum didn't even ask what Margaret wanted to show me, Alice thought, accepting it. She's not interested in me at all. She just wants me to come back when it's time to help with something.

It makes it easier, actually. If Mum doesn't ask questions it's going to make it ever so much easier to see Harry . . . Like that business with Miranda . . . First I thought I could keep it all, but I don't know now. Perhaps if you have one thing, it always means you can't have something else.

Alice rang the bell at Number 27. She had a 'thankyou' present for Margaret – a painting-by-numbers picture, given to her last Christmas and

79

only recently finished. It was the best thing she could find.

Margaret accepted the gift with an enthusiastic show of pleasure. Her smile was full of sunshine, warm as the summer day – but was there something slightly, very slightly uneasy about it? 'Is Harry all right?' Alice asked, suddenly anxious.

'Oh yes! Come in and see!'

Alice followed Margaret over the squiggly brown pattern of the hall carpet, and on to the orange and yellow squiggles of the living room one. There were squiggles all over the walls as well. On the sofa was a blue carry-cot, gleaming softly with newness; and sitting beside the cot, gazing into it with his dull red eyes, was a long, thin, droopy man – Margaret's poor depressed husband, Bill. Bill was so sad that usually looking at him made Alice quite sad too, only at this moment she couldn't feel sad about anything. 'Is Harry asleep?' she whispered.

'I've just put him down.' Margaret's voice quivered with joy. 'Go and have a peep.'

Holding her breath, Alice tiptoed across. The baby lay spread-eagled, breathing lightly and peacefully. He was dressed in a brand-new baby suit, blue and white, with a little frilly collar. 'Bill can't stop looking at him,' said Margaret, round-eyed with delight. The room was so full of love you could feel it.

'I don't want to wake him,' said Alice, wistfully. 'But I would like to cuddle him!'

Margaret lifted the baby, oh so gently, out of his cot. 'Sit in the armchair,' she told Alice. Alice sat, and Margaret placed the baby in her arms. He

80

gave one slightly deeper breath, but didn't open his eyes. Alice bent to kiss his forehead, smelling the warm, sweet, milky smell of him.

It's worth it, she thought, fervently. It's worth terrible yesterday, it's worth all the lies I've had to tell, even that dreadful one I said to Edward. I don't even care about losing Miranda too much, as long as I can keep Harry.

He's mine! He's my baby, he's *mine*!

6

Burglary

Edward fiddled with his computer, but somehow he couldn't concentrate. There was a nasty uneasy feeling in the pit of his stomach, that wouldn't go away. It wasn't my fault the baby died, he told himself, it *wasn't*. It was Alice's fault for not looking after it properly, and I'm not going to think about it any more, I'm *not*.

After a while, he wandered downstairs to see what Grandma was doing.

'Hullo,' said Grandma, cheerfully. 'Want to do this for me? See if I've won anything!'

'I didn't know you went in for scratch cards, Grandma.'

'Only now and again ... Don't tell your father, he's sure to disapprove.' Grandma grinned, a lovely sly grin that showed all the spaces in her teeth – the ones she couldn't be bothered to go to the dentist to have filled in.

Edward took the card. 'What do I have to do with it?'

'Well – you scratch away the top bit, and see what the numbers are underneath. If you get three the same, you've won a prize.'

'It says you can win up to twenty thousand pounds!'

'The fun is in winning, not how *much* you win.

Get on with it then, scratch! Don't keep me in suspense!'

Edward scratched. 'There's three twenties on this one.'

'*What?*'

'There's a one, and two tens, and three twenties – look!'

'Bingo! My stars *were* right today. An unexpected windfall, they said; there's one in the eye for your father! Pity we can't tell him – I've won twenty pounds!'

Grandma beamed her delight. The little monkey face was creased with smiles, the small bright eyes twinkling with glee.

'Why do you think Dad would disapprove?' Edward asked.

'Well – you know, gambling! He thinks gambling is a sin. And a waste of money.'

'I think it's fun,' said Edward. 'What are you going to do with the twenty pounds?'

Grandma considered. 'Well now – first I have to take the ticket back to the shop, of course, for them to give me my prize. And then – then – well, how about some take-away Chinese for supper tonight? Save me having to cook... Of course, we'll have to think of a story for your father.'

Edward was a bit disappointed that Grandma hadn't offered to give him any of her winnings; but never mind – Chinese was a treat, and an exciting idea was beginning to form in his mind. Why hadn't he thought of scratch cards before? He'd slipped up there! 'How much do scratch cards cost?' he asked, carefully casual. No need to let Grandma know what was in his mind; even

Grandma might try to stop him, you never could tell.

'Only a pound,' said Grandma, defensively. 'And it's my money . . . It's not like I'm taking the food out of your mouths, is it?'

Edward could not wait for her to go. As the front door slammed, he ran up to his room, and turned out his little store of savings. Thirty-seven pounds altogether. And Grandma had won twenty pounds with just one ticket! What was twenty times thirty-seven? Of course it didn't work like that, he knew it didn't work like that really. You don't always win . . . But on the other hand, you can win a lot more than twenty pounds . . .

A pound each, Grandma had said. He could spare five. He could risk five, and he would! He listened for Grandma coming back, then slipped out of the house and ran to the shop himself.

'Five scratch cards, please.'

Mr Patel, behind the till, shook his head. 'Sorry. I can't sell scratch cards to you. Sorry.'

'Why not?'

'Against the law. I'm not allowed to sell scratch cards to anyone under sixteen.'

'Oh.'

It was a bitter disappointment, and really not fair, Edward thought. Why must the adults keep all the best things for themselves? And why were all his ideas for making money going wrong? First the baby, and now this! He dawdled outside the shop, trying to think of a way round the problem.

Sixteen. Now who did he know round here who was sixteen? Edward looked hopefully up and down the road. People from the secondary school, perhaps, people on their way home. He knew one or two of them by name, not well, but well enough, perhaps . . . Where were they, though? Any other day, they would be coming in their hordes, swinging their school bags, and taking up all the pavement. Today, when it was really important, they were nowhere to be seen. Come to think of it, the time was getting a bit late. Probably they were all home by now.

Ah – there was one! Going into the shop just now, gangly and spotty, he must be at least sixteen! Edward didn't know him, but that didn't matter. When the boy came out of the shop, Edward would approach him. 'Excuse me,' he would say. 'Buy five pounds' worth of scratch cards for me, and we'll share if I win. Half and half.' No, that was too much – a quarter for him, and three-quarters for Edward . . . No, that was still too much . . .

The spotty boy came out of the shop. Edward followed him, still trying to decide what proportion of the winnings he could get away with offering.

The boy turned into Almond Avenue. Edward felt slightly sick, but kept on going. Nothing to be scared of in Almond Avenue, he told himself. Nothing to get upset about, it wasn't *my* fault the baby died. It was Alice's fault, she didn't look after it properly . . .

Only he was right outside Alice's house now! The one with a statue thing in the front garden, he remembered it clearly. And somewhere in that garden was . . .

The boy ahead was going into a house down the road. Bad luck, I've missed my chance, Edward thought. Never mind, I can find someone with a big brother, can't I? Why didn't I think of that before? Or a sister or something. Somebody at school, tomorrow, it doesn't have to be today.

Edward turned, to make his way back – and stopped short in his tracks. A look of horror came over his face, and he gulped. That's a baby I can hear, isn't it? Sounds like *my* baby! Do babies have ghosts . . . ?

There was another sound – the sound of a window being closed. Not in Alice's house, the house next door. Where those people lived that were home all day it must be. Margaret. Or Mary, was it? And her husband. The ones who couldn't have taken his baby because his baby was dead . . .

Hang about, hang *about*!

Suddenly there was a lump of excitement in Edward's throat. Could it be . . . ?

Oh, but Alice was so sure the baby was dead; she buried it herself, she said so . . .

But that wasn't what she said first! First she said the baby had been stolen, and afterwards she said it was dead . . .

Why did she say that if it wasn't true?

I know what! Ha, ha, I bet I know what happened! I bet Alice sold the baby. I bet she copied my idea and sold it to that Mary, or Margaret or whatever her name is, and told a lie so she could keep all the money for herself. Well, she's not going to get away with that! I've a good mind to knock at her house right now, and tell her I found out her trick!

Careful though, Edward, careful! You have to be careful where you say things. You never know who might be listening, and it still might be against the law to keep a baby, I don't really know about that. Anyway, first find out if what I think is true.

Next morning, Edward managed to waylay Alice on the way to school. Thank goodness she wasn't with that pea-brain Miranda, today. He swung into step beside her. 'Hi!'

Nervous, and dismayed that Edward was still pestering her, Alice walked on without answering.

'How are you feeling? After – you know!'

'I thought we weren't going to talk about that any more.' Why didn't he just go away? Alice willed him to go away, and leave her alone, but he chattered on relentlessly.

'Yeah, I know, but – I just wondered how you were feeling.'

'All right.'

That was a funny thing to say, Edward thought. If *he* had buried a dead baby in the garden, he wouldn't be feeling all right at all. But then, maybe she hadn't buried the baby at all. Ha, ha – she gave herself away there! Carefully offhand, he spoke. 'Actually I've been thinking quite a lot about babies, just lately. You know, people that have babies and people that don't. Things like that.'

Alice felt the panic rising. She swallowed hard and said nothing.

'And I got to thinking – you know that Mary, and whatsisname, her husband. The ones that live next door to you, do *they* have a baby?'

'You mean Margaret and Bill? No.'

'Are you sure?'

'Of course I'm sure. Margaret said she'd have

liked one but she wasn't lucky... Why are you asking me that?'

Edward squinted sideways at Alice, to see if she seemed worried about this conversation, but her face was as blank as usual.

'No reason, just wondering.'

Leanne was stirring up feeling against Alice. It wasn't Alice who had harmed her – stolen Rebecca from under her nose – that was Miranda. But Miranda was too pretty, and too successful, to be picked on, so Leanne vented her spite on Alice. Alice was a crawler, Leanne claimed. Alice was Miss Churchwood's toady. Leanne gathered a following around her, happy to be reassured that they were 'in', by seeing that someone else was 'out'.

Alice did not understand why people were suddenly whispering about her, sniggering when she approached. Even Patsy and Claire seemed uneasy in her company. She was hurt, but not too much. They were nothing but shadows, after all, these whisperers – nothing but ghosts; only Harry was real. At playtime Alice found a corner all by herself, where she could dream about Harry in peace.

For a moment she remembered about Edward, and his disturbing questions that morning, but she pushed that thought away.

'What's this going in to Margaret's all the time?' said Mum, with a hint of peevishness in her voice. 'Something wrong with your home here?'

'No, of course not,' said Alice. 'Margaret was

showing me some photographs, that's all. Of her caravan . . . I wish we had a caravan, for holidays.'

'We don't need a caravan. We go to Majorca.'

'I know, but—'

'And what about helping with William's bath? You used to enjoy that.'

'I'll be back in time. I will, Mum, I promise.'

Edward had waited impatiently for school to finish. Only one thing more to find out, now. Margaret and Bill had no baby of their own, so if there *was* a baby at their house it had to be his, it stood to reason!

Now what excuse could he make, for knocking at the door?

Edward made his way warily down Almond Avenue. He didn't want Alice to see him. He didn't want Alice to know his suspicions; he wanted to find out for certain if he was right, first.

Halfway down the road he stopped. But that *was* Alice, wasn't it? Coming out of her own house and going in next door, if he wasn't much mistaken! Edward dodged behind a tree. Ha, ha, he'd caught her now, hadn't he? Going to collect her money from Margaret and Bill. *His* money!

Alice hadn't buried the baby in the garden, had she? He always thought there was something funny about that, she was too soft . . . But he never would have guessed she could be crafty either . . .

Once she had disappeared, Edward almost ran. But no, no, be careful! If they knew he was on to them they could hide it, perhaps – Alice and Margaret and Bill all ganging up together to cheat him. He must be as crafty and cunning as they were . . .

He knew what he had to do, to make absolutely certain; and it was going to be difficult, and dangerous, and very, very exciting. He noted the number of the house carefully, to leave no possible room for mistakes later – Number 27.

Bill was helping with the nappy change. Bill had come to life in the most amazing way. His little red eyes had a light in them now. 'Look, James,' said Bill. 'Here's Aunty Alice, come to see you!'

'James?' said Alice, puzzled. 'You mean Harry, don't you?'

'Of course he does,' said Margaret, not quite easily.

'And I'm not his aunty, I'm his mummy.'

'Of course you are,' Margaret reassured her.

'Can I hold him now?'

'Well – he's had his feed and he's a bit sleepy . . .'

'But I've waited all day. He wants his mummy to hold him, doesn't he? He must have missed me, he must have!'

'I'm sure he has,' said Margaret, with a bright smile that didn't look quite right.

Edward had waited till dark. Because it was the middle of summer, he had had to wait a long time. He was in bed, because nine o'clock was his bedtime, and Dad was strict about that; but Dad didn't know that Edward, obediently under the sheet, still had his daytime clothes on.

Ha, ha, this was going to be fun! Outwitting Dad, and Grandma, and all of them!

Oddly, though, now the time had come, Edward wasn't altogether sure he wanted to go. Correction – it had to be admitted, he didn't really want to go at all. But he had decided it, he had planned it; if he chickened out now, he would never respect himself again.

Dad and Grandma would be in the sitting room now, watching television. All Edward had to do was to tiptoe down the stairs, open the front door quietly, and close the latch with his key. No noise, easy peasy! Cautiously, he slipped out of bed and opened the door of his room.

There! He had done it, he was in the street! *Now* all he had to do was run round to Almond Avenue, and find Number 27.

There was a light in the downstairs front room, as Edward had expected there to be. There were lights downstairs in nearly all the houses. Everybody watching television, Margaret and Bill included. The baby, he reasoned, would be upstairs.

He must get into the house, and creep up the stairs, and find his baby, and then he would know.

It was a pity he didn't actually want to do it . . . It was a pity his legs had gone weak, and somebody had put a cold hand into his chest, to squeeze his heart with . . . It was a pity that what he most wanted to do, right now, was to run back to his own house, and get back to bed before anyone noticed he had gone.

. . . And never respect himself again!

Come on, Edward, come on! The back door, like you planned. Margaret and Bill haven't gone to bed yet, so it won't be locked . . .

Edward glanced swiftly up and down the road, but there was no one to see him. In his soft-soled trainers, he ran round the side of the house. His heart was thumping, and he had to stop to get his breath, even though he hadn't run very far. He was sweating a bit too, he discovered. Most likely because it was such a warm night. He tried the back door.

It *was* locked!

Now what did they do that for? What did they go and do that for? Edward went to the window, and tried to peer through, but the kitchen was in darkness.

The window, however, had not been properly shut.

It was one of those push-out windows, the sort that would not be at all easy to climb through. Could he? Dared he? His heart was thumping so hard now it must surely burst out of his chest. The window was quite high – probably over the sink. Edward put both hands underneath and lifted it.

There was room; there would be room to crawl through if he could get himself high enough. Edward put his hands on the sill, and hoisted his long slim body.

He was through.

His hands were grasping the far edge of the sink, and he was dragging himself into the kitchen. He was doing it, he was actually doing it, it was like a dream!

And suddenly, the light in the kitchen snapped on!

Edward had time to notice blue work tops, and a red floor with a squiggly blue design on it. He had time to notice those things as he slithered backwards through the window, and time to hear a frightened scream: 'Margaret, come! Margaret, COME!'

Edward dropped to the ground and began to run.

He ran round the side of the house, and into the road, pelting for home. At any moment, he expected to find a great big policeman barring his way. 'Are you the intruder in Almond Avenue?' the stern voice would say. 'Just come along to the station with me, young man!' There was even a siren – oh, horror of horrors a *police car*, in the distance! Coming to get him for certain! Edward dived into someone's front garden and crouched behind a hedge until he could be sure that the police car had gone a different way . . . Still looking for him, though, it was only a matter of time . . .

He was home! He was safe in his own front garden! The light was out in the front room, which meant Dad and Grandma would have gone to bed already. This was awkward, of course; he would have to be very careful going up the stairs. He turned his two keys in the locks.

Push, rattle!

Of course, of course, how could he have forgotten? On going to bed, Dad always put the chain on the door as well as locking it! The back door would certainly be locked and bolted as well.

So what now?

His own bedroom window was open, but what use was that? There was a drainpipe, the street light showed him, passing not too far from his bedroom window . . . Could he climb it? He had

never attempted any such thing, but perhaps . . .
Edward grasped the pipe, and tried to haul himself
up.

His fingers stung, and his knuckles scraped painfully against the stonework. He braced his feet
against the wall of the house, and tried to move
upwards.

No use, his arms were not strong enough.

Now he was really frightened. Either he must
spend the night in the garden, it seemed, and be
discovered anyway the next day, or he must rouse
the household, and face Dad's anger straight away.

Panicky now, he made another assault on the
drainpipe. He *could* do it, he *would* do it! He
struggled and hauled himself a little further up
the front wall of the house.

More, more, he must climb higher! Edward
looked up, to see how far he had come, and was
dismayed to find how much farther he had to go.
Well, he couldn't do it, and that was that. All this
pain was ridiculous, he wasn't prepared to stand
another moment of it. He loosed his grip and fell.

More pain – his foot this time, so excruciatingly
sharp that he couldn't help crying out.

Lights. And running footsteps. And Dad in his
nightwear, come to catch the burglar. For the
second time that night, Edward was a burglar. It
was getting to be a habit; it was almost funny.
Edward forced his mouth into a wry grin, begging
Dad to see the funny side. 'It's only me!'

'What are you doing there, you idiot?'

'Only a bit of fun.'

Dad was not amused. 'Yes, well basically your bit

of fun is keeping everyone from getting their sleep, but I don't expect you to think of that! Get up!'

Edward tried, but a stab of agony shot through his ankle. He yelled. 'I think I broke my foot.'

'You're lucky you didn't break your neck!' Dad lifted him, none too gently, and half carried him into the house. 'As if I hadn't enough to worry about!'

Grandma was in the hall, in her dressing gown; she did her best to avert attention from the crime. 'Look at his leg, he's hurt.' Nice one, Grandma!

'He deserves to be hurt,' said Dad, grimly.

'That ankle needs a cold compress, though.'

'Basically, it's his head I'm worried about, not his ankle. Eleven years old, and already out on the tiles. Or whatever. Where *have* you been, Edward?'

'I went to see my girlfriend,' said Edward, with sudden inspiration.

'You *what?*'

'I went to see my girlfriend.'

Dad laughed. 'Come on, you don't expect me to believe that!'

'Why not?'

'*You?* With a girlfriend?'

What was that supposed to mean? Edward had a moment of horrible self-doubt – was there something wrong with him? Was he not good-looking enough, perhaps? I could have a girlfriend if I wanted one, he assured himself. I just don't want one, that's all.

'Are you in a gang by any chance?' Dad persisted. 'Are you on drugs?'

'*No!*'

'Joyriding?'

'NO!'

Edward was bewildered. So many crimes a person could commit, and he'd never thought of doing any of them.

'All right,' said Dad, suddenly tired. 'We'll leave it till the morning . . .'

Oh joy and jubilation! By morning, with luck, Dad might have forgotten all about it. Dad had a lot of worries; with any luck Dad's worries would keep him too busy to remember.

Later, curled up in bed, Edward tried to still the racing thoughts. At this rate he would *never* get to sleep. All that fuss and bother he put himself through, and nothing gained at the end of it . . . Suddenly there was a picture in his mind. A sharp, clear picture of a kitchen, painfully red and blue . . . and something on the worktop beside the sink. Something important. What? Oh yes, yes, *he* knew what it was! Ha, ha, he knew what that was all right! Funny he hadn't properly noticed it before but never mind, the picture had saved itself for him, to show itself to him, in the quiet darkness now when he would realise what it meant.

It was a baby's bottle!

7

Betrayed!

There was something wrong. Alice couldn't put her finger on it, but tonight, going into Number 27, Alice felt the wrongness.

No less love, it wasn't that. Harry, pink and white, clean and sweet-smelling, lay in his carrycot while the love washed over him in waves. But there was a feeling in the air of the rooms – something sharp, and prickly, a kind of tingling, as though something might be going to go off pop at any time, like a bottle of Coke that gets opened too quickly.

Upstairs in the bathroom, Alice felt the prickliness on her skin, and catching in her throat when she breathed. It's coming from Margaret, she thought; Margaret has swallowed a bomb and it's going to explode in a minute! She brushed that silly thought away and held the wonder, the soft newly bathed miracle, against her cheek. 'I can't believe he's mine, I can't believe it!'

'Let's get him dried before he catches cold,' said Margaret.

There was an edge to Margaret's voice, as though she was forcing the words. There was something wrong with her smile as well – as though she was *making* the smile, not just letting it come naturally. Perhaps Margaret wasn't feeling very well. She looked tired, now Alice came to notice, as though she had been up all night. Perhaps Harry had been crying. Perhaps Margaret had a headache; oh, poor Margaret! 'Have you got a headache, Margaret?' Alice asked.

'No, no. What makes you say that?'

'I don't know . . .'

'Let's get him downstairs for his feed.'

There was something different from usual about the landing. What was it? Oh yes, the *doors* were shut. In this house the doors were always open, always – different squiggles in every room, all proudly open to view. But this evening the doors were closed . . .

Saturday at last! Alice had thought it would never come. All day, all day to see Harry!

'Why don't you pack a suitcase?' said Mum. 'Then you could move in next door permanently.'

'I won't be long . . . Bill wants to tell me about when he was in the war.'

'In the war? What war?'

'I don't know. Just the war.'

'Anyway, what's happened to Miranda these days? You two fell out?'

Alice thought she might as well agree that they had; it would save awkward questions in future. 'Miranda isn't my best friend any more, she's Rebecca's best friend.'

'Ho, hum. You don't sound too upset about it. One time you seemed to be joined at the hip.'

'She's silly,' said Alice. 'She giggles too much.'

Mum laughed her little fluting laugh. 'Well, what's wrong with that? Anyway, I've heard *you* giggling with Miranda a few times.'

'Not any more,' said Alice. She had grown-up responsibilities now, hadn't she, she had a baby! 'It's childish.'

'Well, get you!' Mum laughed.

Alice rang the bell at Number 27, and waited for Margaret or Bill to come to the door. She thought about how amazingly Bill had changed; it was Harry who had changed him. When I take Harry back, to be my very own, Alice thought, I'll let Bill see him as much as he wants, so he will go on being happy. She pictured the scene. 'Here's Uncle Bill come to see you. Say hullo to Uncle Bill . . . Oh dear, he's a bit shy today.' It occurred to her, for a moment, that she had no idea how she ever *was* going to take Harry back, but she pushed that thought away.

They were taking a long time answering the door. Alice rang again.

Nothing.

She pushed the letter-box open, and peered into the hall. Empty, quiet, dead almost. Alice wandered round to the back of the house. The back door was locked, and the kitchen window was shut fast. The garage was locked as well, so she couldn't see if Margaret's little red car was there or not. I suppose they've gone shopping, she thought. Funny, though, they didn't tell me. They knew I was coming.

She went back to her own house, and watched through the window of William's room to see if the car came back. It didn't, so Alice went back to Number 27 to ring the bell again.

Nothing.

She looked through the bay window, into the

front sitting room, and immediately saw that there was something different. The photographs! The photographs that stood on the bookshelf, the ones of Margaret's parents and Bill's parents – the photographs were missing! What could it mean?

Alice went home, and stood about disconsolately, unsure what to do next. 'Thought you were going round to Margaret's,' said Mum.

'They seem to be out.'

'Doing their shopping I suppose.'

'Yes . . .'

Alice tried again just after lunch, but Number 27 was still quiet and deserted. 'How about a family outing?' said Dad. 'How about we all get in the car, and whizz off to Richmond? Have a couple of hours by the river.'

'I don't want to,' said Alice.

'Pudding! You always want to!' said Dad, astonished.

'Well I don't now.'

'Is she getting a mind of her own or something?' said Dad.

They went to Richmond, and sat by the river, and smelled the hot smells of summer. They watched the boats going up and down, while the sun made dancing patterns, on the water. They ate ice creams – rainbow-coloured ones that slid over their chins in cold, sweet trickles. At any other time this would have been heaven, but today it was all spoiled for Alice by a nagging worry that wouldn't go away. What had happened to Margaret and Bill? Why hadn't they told her they were going to be out this morning and this afternoon? Where had they gone?

A horrible thought came into her mind. Perhaps they had had an accident in Margaret's car! Perhaps Harry had been hurt... or worse! In sharp and sickening detail, Alice pictured the mangled red car, the twisted up bits inside, the baby. Oh, she couldn't wait, she couldn't wait, for this afternoon to be over, so she could get back to Almond Avenue, and see if Margaret and Bill had come back yet...

When they were nearly home, William was a little bit sick in his car seat, and Alice sitting next to him was busy mopping him up, so she wasn't the first to see it. 'Well, what do you know!' said Dad. 'Just look at that! HAW, HAW, HAW!'

Planted in the front garden of Number 27 was a brand new estate agent's sign. The sign said FOR SALE.

'They're moving!' said Mum. 'Did they say anything to you about that, Alice?'

'No.'

She couldn't believe it. There must be some explanation, but what? Alice flung herself out of the car, and ran to the front door of Number 27. 'It's not that important!' Mum called after her. 'Aren't you going to help me with William?'

Number 27 was still empty. Peering through the letter-box once more, Alice was aware of a sort of lifeless chill inside. Margaret's house has died, she thought in dismay. While we were at Richmond Margaret's house has gone and died!

'Not there?' said Dad, cheerfully. 'Be back later, I expect.'

Dad must be right, Alice thought, he *must*!

Sunday morning came, and Margaret and Bill were still not back. 'They'll have to come back some time,' said Dad, 'to get their stuff.'

'Perhaps they took it already,' Mum suggested. 'Perhaps they've emptied the house.'

'They haven't,' said Alice. 'I looked.'

'Are you *sure* they didn't say anything to you, Alice?' said Mum.

Alice shook her head. 'I don't understand it. I was supposed to go in yesterday morning.'

'Gone to their caravan for a few days, I expect,' said Mum.

'But not without telling *me*,' Alice protested. 'When they knew I was coming!'

'Perhaps they were called away suddenly,' was Dad's idea. 'Family crisis or something.'

'They haven't *got* any family,' said Alice. 'Their family are all dead.'

'That's right,' said Mum. 'They got all the lolly from both sets of parents. That's why they don't have money worries.' She sighed, smiling happily, and added 'Lucky things!' not meaning it for a minute.

'Perhaps one of them's ill,' Dad went on. 'And the other one's at the bedside. In a hospital somewhere . . . Funny about the FOR SALE thing-ummy though.'

'They didn't tell me!' said Alice, desperately. 'Why didn't they tell me?'

'Oh, Alice,' said Mum. 'You aren't that important!'

'*I* know what it is,' said Dad, over the ham salad on Monday evening. '*I* know what it is, they've done a runner!'

'What do you mean?' said Alice, though she had a horrible queasy feeling in the pit of her stomach, that Dad was right.

'Well – they've got on the wrong side of the law, haven't they? Maybe Bill robbed a bank! HAW, HAW, HAW! At gunpoint!'

'Last time I saw him,' said Mum, 'he hadn't the strength to lift his knife and fork, let alone a gun.'

'All right – Margaret was caught shoplifting! Stealing frilly undies from Marks and Sparks! HAW, HAW, HAW!'

Mum giggled. '*Margaret*? In *frilly undies*? The mind boggles!'

'OK, OK, how about this? One of them's murdered the other, and buried the body somewhere in the back garden. HAW, HAW, HAW!'

'I don't think that's funny,' said Alice.

'Good lord, Pudding, what's happened to your sense of humour?' said Dad.

Alice took another mouthful of supper, tried to swallow it, and felt it rising in a lump to choke her. 'I feel sick,' she announced through clenched teeth, as she rushed for the bathroom.

'Not again!' said Mum. 'I thought we finished with that!'

Alice sat on the lavatory seat, and let the thoughts come – the thoughts she had been trying so hard for the last two days to hide from herself.

They had cheated her!

Margaret and Bill, who had pretended to be her friends, had cheated her. She was never going to see Harry again, because Margaret and Bill had run away with him. They were not coming back, not to get their stuff or anything. They had run away with Harry, to keep him all for themselves.

They had probably planned it from the beginning. Or *Margaret* had planned it. Margaret had never meant that Harry should be Alice's; Alice had just been used. They had let her come in to cuddle Harry, and bath him and so on, just to keep her happy while they made their plans.

Oh, how could she have been so stupid!

How could she have thought that a baby could be kept hidden, even inside Margaret's house? Not for long, anyway – babies grow up. She had believed it because she wanted to believe it; she saw that now, and she didn't feel grown-up any more, she felt silly. She felt silly, and she felt betrayed.

Margaret had lied to her. She had trusted Margaret with the most precious thing in her life; and Margaret had lied to her, and taken that precious thing away. Alice was devastated. In the whole of her life she was never, ever going to get over this!

Edward sprawled over the couch, resting his sprained ankle, and brooding.

As he had hoped, Dad seemed to have forgotten there was an unsolved mystery about Edward's injury. That was all right – Dad did seem to forget about Edward quite often, when his worries got really bad. Dad had a lot of worries, mostly about money. Edward, of course, did not intend to have any worries about money, because he was going to be a millionaire.

The big question now was – how was he going to achieve this?

There were two possibilities, at the moment. Get the money that was rightfully due to him for his baby. Or win a fortune on the scratch cards. Unfortunately, since he was just now confined to the house, there was nothing to be done about either of them for the moment. Edward fretted, impatiently. Tuesday already – was the whole week going to be wasted like this?

Grandma came in from the kitchen. There was a delicious herby smell, poking its way into every corner of the house; one of Grandma's casseroles. 'Shall we find your stars?' Grandma suggested.

'If you like,' said Edward, not really interested.

Grandma rustled through the paper. 'Here we are – Capricorn. *An unexpected windfall.*'

'That's what it said for you, the other day.'

'Yes,' said Grandma, triumphantly. 'And look how right they were!'

'It's all very well for you,' said Edward, bitterly. 'You're over sixteen.'

'I'm over *sixty* – what's that got to do with it?'

'They won't sell scratch cards to people under sixteen.'

'Oh – I see . . .' Grandma looked thoughtful. 'It would be a pity to waste good stars . . .'

Edward stared at her. '*Grandma*! You *wouldn't*!'

'Well, I know I *shouldn't.*'

'I was going to find somebody's big brother.'

'Risky,' said Grandma.

'You mean, because they might cheat? And keep the money for themselves?'

'Much better to keep it in the family.'

Edward could hardly believe what he was hearing. But then, he had always known Grandma wasn't like other adults. 'What about Dad?'

'He doesn't have to know.' Grandma looked at the clock. 'Only five o'clock. A good hour before he gets back. Of course, I know I shouldn't . . .' She was looking rather like a naughty child – excited and shamefaced both at the same time.

'If I tell you where to find five pounds, will you get it for me?' said Edward, his own excitement mounting. 'And buy the tickets?'

Grandma hesitated. 'That's a lot of money, Edward!'

She went, nevertheless, and returned grinning and waving a strip of them. 'I got five in a row, all the same type,' she explained. 'One of them's almost sure to be a winner . . . Of course, the prize might be only a pound.'

Edward understood. It would hurt to lose his five pounds, so carefully saved, but that was the chance you took. He took the cards and began to scratch . . .

' . . . Grandma! I've won *fifty pounds*!'

'Are you sure?'

'Look!'

Grandma was as excited as Edward. 'What did I tell you? What did I tell you about the stars?'

'Will you get my fifty pounds for me?'

'Yes . . .'

There was hesitation in Grandma's voice. 'You *will* get them for me won't you?' said Edward.

'Yes . . . Unless . . .'

'*Grandma!*'

'I was going to say . . .' Grandma turned her head, looking even more like a naughty child. 'I was going to say . . . Unless you'd like to make a bit more fun out of it . . .'

'How?'

'I shall be punished. For even suggesting such a thing.'

'Suggesting *what?*'

'Well – supposing, instead of getting fifty pounds . . . supposing we got, say, twenty-five pounds and *twenty-five more tickets?*'

Edward's mouth opened and stayed open. Suddenly there was a firework display going on in his head – coloured wheels giddily spinning, shooting rockets, the lot! He hesitated. 'What about the stars?'

'We could wait till they're right . . .'

'Let's do that! Let's do that, Grandma!'

The waiting would be agony, of course. How long would it have to be? Days? Weeks even, perhaps! And he wanted it all to be *now.* Never mind, he could spend the time thinking about how wonderful his life was going to be.

He was on his way to being a millionaire, at last he was truly on his way! With the stars on his side, how could he fail? Twenty-five tickets? That could mean hundreds, even thousands of pounds in prizes. And there could be more tickets after that. And more, and more. And more and more prizes, hundreds and thousands of pounds . . .

He could forget about the baby. The baby was just a nuisance, he didn't need the baby now.

'Still no sign of Margaret and Bill,' said Mum. 'I'm beginning to think we won't see them again.'

'Police don't seem interested anyway,' said Dad, sounding almost regretful. 'They haven't been round asking questions, have they?'

Alice felt a stab of new fear. 'Do you think they will, then? Do you think the police might really come?'

Dad shook his head. 'Only if they think they're on to 'em for something. No law against moving house without telling anybody, so far as I know!'

And I'm the only one who knows what Margaret and Bill *really* did, Alice thought bitterly. And they know I won't tell because of getting into trouble myself. Anyway, thank goodness I don't have to worry about the police!

Emily slumped into the armchair, after an exhausting day at school. 'What's the matter with you?' her mum asked, not for the first time.

'Nothing,' said Emily, trying to smile.

'You're as pale as a ghost. I think you've lost weight as well.' Emily's mother regarded with concern the bloodless cheeks; the eyes once bright with eagerness and fun – now dull, with dark rings round them; the lank, neglected hair. 'Your dad and I are a bit worried about you, you know!'

'Oh, don't fuss!'

'I wonder if you're anaemic.'

'I'm not anaemic, I'm fine.'

'You're *not* fine; I think we should go down the doctor's. This evening.'

Emily panicked. 'No, not the doctor's, not the doctor's!'

'Why not? What are you frightened of?'

'Nothing. There's nothing wrong with me.' Emily forced her mouth into a sickly grin, and leaped to her feet with all the energy she could muster, to prove how perfectly all right she was. But the sudden movement made her giddy; her head swam so she had to sit down again. Her mother looked long and hard, then took a deep breath.

'Emily . . .'

Emily leaned her elbows on her knees, her gaze fixed on the floor. 'What now?'

'Look – don't be afraid to tell me . . . You aren't . . . by any chance . . . *pregnant*, are you?'

Emily laughed a harsh laugh. '*No!*'

'You're not even afraid you might be?'

'Mum, I promise you, there's no chance of that in the world!'

'Well, that's a relief . . .'

8

Bullied!

Alice was confused. Why was no one talking to her? The sniggering and whispering of last week hadn't mattered much, because then she had Harry. But this silence mattered a great deal. This silence was one more shattering thing that had come out of the blue to knock her down, down, to somewhere below the ground.

Even Patsy and Claire had been getting less and less friendly; and today, Wednesday, it seemed they preferred to pretend she wasn't there. If Alice said: 'Can I borrow your rubber?' Patsy turned her head and spoke to Lucy on the other side. If Alice offered to share her felt tip pens with Claire, Claire seemed not to hear, but asked Flora for hers, instead.

At playtime, things suddenly became worse than ever. Alice had retreated to a corner, where she could nurse her wretchedness in peace. She was in a deep dark hole, or so it seemed. She was all by herself in this deep dark hole, with the anguish of losing Harry still a crushing weight in her chest – and now this bewildering, devastating thing that no one would talk to her.

What could it all be about?

Someone was coming towards her. It was Leanne, smiling but not pleasantly. It was Leanne with a spiteful smirk on her face; coming towards

Alice with outstretched hand – outstretched hand which grabbed a lock of Alice's hair and tugged excruciatingly. Alice yelped.

'That's for being Miss Churchwood's sneak!' Leanne taunted her.

'What do you mean?'

'You're always telling tales to Miss Churchwood, to get us in trouble.'

Alice was astounded. 'I'm *not*!'

The accusation was totally unfounded, and most of the girls in Leanne's gang must have known this, in their hearts. But it was fun to have a victim, and Leanne had provided them with one. They were all around Alice now, a gang of them, jeering. 'Sneak! Crawler!'

Not everyone was in the gang. Patsy and Claire, for instance, were carefully distancing themselves from the mob. It was unwise to go against powerful people like Leanne; if you did that you might find you were getting picked on yourself. But you were reasonably safe not actually joining in.

And Miranda was not there. Miranda was in a far corner of the playground with Rebecca, interested only in Rebecca. She was not feeling entirely comfortable; it was impossible to be totally unaware of what was going on, and there was no way harmless Alice could have deserved what was happening to her, was there? But this was not Miranda's fault. It was nothing to do with her, was it? There was no reason in the world she should feel she ought to go to Alice's rescue, was there?

Trembling, Alice turned her face to the wall, leaning her forehead against the rough stone, hands over her ears to block out the ugly sounds.

'Go away! Leave me alone!' In her mind's eye she saw her tormentors still, their pointing fingers grown long and skinny, their mouths full of needle-sharp teeth, like a lot of witches.

They must have gone, though, or maybe the teacher on duty had shooed them away, because when Alice dared to turn round she found she was all by herself in her deep dark hole again.

At home time her bag was missing. They stood around in the cloakroom watching her look for it. 'What's the matter, Alice?' said Leanne. 'Lost something?'

'You've taken it, haven't you?' said Alice. 'What have you done with it?'

'*Me?* Take your bag? What would I want your bag for?'

Alice's throat tightened, so she could not answer.

'Nobody wants *your* bag, Alice,' said Flora, grinning.

There was a lot of unkind laughter, and Miss Churchwood came into the cloakroom to see what it was all about. 'Is anything wrong?' she wanted to know.

Alice could have told Miss Churchwood about the missing bag, but didn't want to be accused of sneaking again. She tucked her homework under her arm and plodded home alone, tears smarting and pricking, blurring her path.

'What happened to your bag?' said Mum.

'I don't know, I lost it,' said Alice. 'I'm sorry.'

She didn't tell Mum about the bullying. That was something too shameful to tell, too humiliating to have to admit. She went to bed that night, and cried in her heart for Harry, until the pain of that loss overshadowed her fears about the morning, and school.

Next day it was her coat. The weather had changed, and was cloudy and a bit chilly, so everyone wore coats to school. Alice hung hers on her peg as usual, and at home time it was missing.

'Didn't you bring a coat today, Alice?' said Flora, giggling.

'She had one this morning,' said Leanne. 'I saw it.'

'Let's all help her to look for it,' someone offered. Amid much sniggering, the girls pretended to hunt for Alice's coat.

'Better find it for her,' Leanne urged. 'Otherwise she'll tell Miss Churchwood we took it.'

'Or her mummy!'

'Ha, ha, ha!'

Alice went home without her coat.

On Friday, Alice had to wear her old coat to school. She was frightened to hang it on her peg in the cloakroom, but more frightened of taking it into class with her, in case Miss Churchwood noticed.

At home time, however, it was her swimming kit that was missing.

'Oh *no*!' said Mum – not really angry, it would be too much trouble to be *really* angry – but showing exasperation which was not like her. 'What's the matter with you, Alice? How can you be losing all these things, what's going on? Is somebody playing tricks on you? Is that what it is?'

'*No*!'

'Well, what then?'

'I didn't really lose them, I just forgot to bring them home.' Surely, *surely*, Alice thought, the things must turn up soon. Leanne must give them back to me soon, Leanne and the others.

'Well mind you do. You're getting really absent-minded, really careless, do you know that?'

'I'm sorry,' said Alice, humbly.

'Yes, well sorry isn't good enough! I don't know what your dad's going to say when I tell him.'

It was a small thing, and Mum wasn't as cross as she might have been. But she wasn't *pleased* any more. 'Can I do some shopping for you?' Alice offered. 'Is there anything we need?'

'No thank you,' Mum said, quite sharply. 'You'll probably forget what you went for. Or lose it on the way back.'

On Monday, Alice gathered all her courage and confronted Leanne. 'I know you've got my things, so please give them back.'

'Did somebody speak?' said Leanne.

'Yes, *I* did. I said, please give my things back.'

'Oh,' said Leanne. 'I thought somebody spoke. I must have imagined it.'

At home time, Alice tried again. 'Leanne, can I have my things back, please?'

'I don't know what you're talking about.'

'Yes you do.'

'Does anybody know what Alice is talking about? No, sorry, Alice, nobody knows.'

Once more, Alice went home in her old coat, carrying her homework under her arm.

She didn't go indoors, but ran straight down the

114

path to the playhouse. No one called after her, so presumably Mum hadn't seen her come in, which was one good thing, because she didn't know, actually, how she was going to manage facing Mum, tonight. Nor Dad neither. 'Come on, Pudding,' he had said last night, not joking at all. 'You pull yourself together, do you hear me?'

Mum and Dad were not pleased with her any more.

And she dared not do things for Miss Churchwood any more, so now Miss Churchwood would not be pleased with her either.

But worst of all, Margaret and Bill had run away. She had trusted them, and they had run away with her baby. She had been silly about the baby, of course, but it was cruel what they did, and how could she ever trust anyone again?

And she had loved Harry so much, and she missed him so much still, but she was never going to see him again, was she?

And Miranda was not her friend any more, indeed she had no friends, had she?

She had nothing . . .

She didn't understand why the girls had all turned against her, but perhaps it *was* somehow her fault.

She wasn't good enough for people to like her, that was it.

She wasn't worth anything.

Really and truly, she would rather not be alive any more. Perhaps, if she wished it hard enough, she wouldn't wake up tomorrow morning . . .

But morning came as usual, and there was school to be faced.

No!

It was too much, she *couldn't* face it. She didn't know what she was going to do, but she knew for certain she was not going to school.

'Don't come home without your things!' Mum called after her, as she left the house.

She couldn't go to school, and she couldn't go home tonight either! Alice wandered into the park, and sat on the first seat she came to, her mind filling up with dreadful thoughts. She thought about the heart-sinking disappointment of waking up this morning when she had wished so hard not to. She thought about other things a person might do, things that would really work, to make sure of going to sleep, and never waking up again, ever . . .

Edward pranced into the park, going to school for the first time since the accident to his foot. He was in great spirits, and not just because his ankle wasn't hurting any more.

Today was the day!

He had been reading the stars himself, in Grandma's daily paper, rushing to pick it off the mat the moment it was delivered. 'An excellent day for all money matters,' was the message for Capricorn, this morning. Well, you couldn't get better than that, and Grandma agreed. So by the time he got back from school she would have them ready for him – his twenty-five pounds, and his twenty-five tickets.

By this evening, he could be richer by a thousand pounds or more! He had not the slightest doubt that he was going to win.

116

There was a soft mist after rain, with the sweet scent of a new day beginning, rising and swirling all around him. Edward leaped and whooped and clapped his hands above his head. What a brilliant, brilliant world to be alive in!

He was vaguely surprised to see Alice, sitting on her seat, but not specially interested. He said 'Hi', to be polite, but she didn't say 'Hi' back, just went on staring, with eyes that didn't appear to see. Edward stopped, and said 'Hi' again.

Alice went on sitting there, not moving, just looking into space. Something about her stillness made Edward feel slightly uncomfortable. 'You coming to school then?' he suggested.

Alice said nothing.

Now Edward felt *really* uncomfortable. 'You all right?' he asked, though it was fairly clear by now that she was not. 'Are you ill or something?'

Alice shook her head.

'What is it, then?'

'. . . Everything's horrible,' she whispered at last.

'Oh.' Edward considered. He could only think of one thing that might have upset her so much. 'Is it anything to do with the baby? I know the baby's not dead. I know you sold it to the people next door.'

Tears rolled down the heavy red cheeks. 'I didn't sell the baby, you can't think that!'

'Oh.' It sounded like the truth, but how could it be? Edward considered. 'How did those people get to have it, then? I know they've got it, you can't say they haven't got it.'

'I didn't sell it to them, though; she found it out.

117

Margaret found it out.' Alice began to sob, great ugly sobs that caught in her throat, and shook her whole body. 'I tried to keep it a secret, but Margaret found it out and took the baby in her house.'

'Do you mean you let her have it for nothing?'

'You don't understand.' She was crying so much now she could hardly speak. 'It wasn't going to be Margaret's baby, it was going to be my baby. Margaret was just looking after him for me.'

'No, no! It couldn't be *your* baby, Alice, it was *my* baby. I found it.'

'I know, but ... Well, yes, I suppose ...' The sobs began to subside, as she struggled to work it out all over again. 'Anyway, they took him away. I don't know where they went. I shall never see him again, shall I?'

'So? What's the difference? He wasn't your baby anyway, he was mine!'

Alice was silent, confused about everything now, feeling the thoughts in her head going round and round. She grabbed at them, trying to still the mad whirling. Edward fidgeted, impatiently.

'Come on then, let's go to school, we're going to be late.'

She began to cry once more. 'I'm not going to school. I'm sorry.'

'What's the matter now?'

She didn't want to tell him. She didn't want to say it out loud, it was too shaming – but the words came tumbling out, almost as if they had a life of their own. 'It's the girls. They're all being horrible to me.' Amazingly, Alice felt quite a bit better now the words had been said at last.

118

'Which girls?'

'A lot of them. Leanne mostly. And Flora, and Lucy.'

'Oh, *them*!' said Edward, contemptuously. 'You don't want to take any notice of *them.*'

'But they've got my things, and they won't give them back. I didn't do anything to them, they just started picking on me.'

Edward knew how it was. He knew how those girls could pick on a person – they had done it to him, hadn't they, only a short while ago! Alice had tried to cheat him – to sell the baby or keep it, it amounted to the same thing – and although the baby wasn't important now, he hadn't yet quite forgiven her. Nevertheless, he began to regard her with new sympathy. Certainly she wasn't tough like he'd once thought – she couldn't be! And girls do get soppy over babies, he thought, so perhaps there's some excuse for what she did. Anyway, I think she understands it now.

'What about Miranda?' he suggested. 'Doesn't she stand up for you?'

'She's not my friend any more.'

'Oh, right . . .' Well, *that* would be no great loss. '*I'll* get your things back for you,' he offered.

'Will you!' She could hardly believe what she was hearing. 'How?'

'I'll find a way. You'll see!' He had no idea, actually, how he was going to achieve any such thing, but it made him feel good to imagine it done. He had a few scores of his own to settle with those girls, hadn't he?

Alice stopped crying, and walked meekly with Edward along the path. She was too shy to look at

119

him, but deep inside her the coldness, the numb despair, was beginning to dissolve. I've got somebody on my side, she thought gratefully. *I've got somebody on my side!*

Edward had mostly gone back to thinking about how rich he was going to be, this evening. Alice Cousins and her troubles were of very small consequence compared with *that*.

As the morning wore on, however, the memory of what he had undertaken to do nagged at him, and Edward began to feel annoyed with himself for making a promise he didn't know how he was going to keep. There was only one way he could think of, and it wasn't a particularly noble one; in fact, some people might say it made him into a tell-tale-tit.

Oh well, who cared what some people might say!

He wasn't keen, he found, to take on a whole gang, but he managed to corner Leanne at playtime. 'You have to give back Alice's things.'

'What things?'

'Don't waste my time pretending you don't know.'

'Get out of my way!'

'When you give back Alice's things.'

'I haven't got her things!'

'If you don't give them back, I'm going to tell Miss Churchwood, and she's going to tell your parents, and you're probably going to get expelled.'

'Ha, ha, ha!'

'I mean it, Leanne!'

She glared at him, with a darkening face. 'You're a nasty sneaky squirt, Edward Lawson, do you know that?'

'I'm not cruel, though. I'm not a bully, like some people I could mention.'

'Oh yes, Saint Edward Lawson! Ha, ha, ha!'

She went off, leaving Edward very much afraid he'd been a tell-tale-tit *and* failed! But towards the end of playtime Leanne reappeared, accompanied this time by a couple of her cronies, carrying an armful of miscellaneous items which she threw at Edward one by one. 'Edward Lawson loves Alice Cousins!' jeered one of the cronies, and the three moved off, elbowing one another and sniggering.

Edward's only wish was to get rid of the embarrassing articles as soon as possible. He found Alice, all alone but not looking *funny* any more, and thrust the bundle into her arms. 'There you are,' he said gruffly. 'They won't try it again!'

He wasn't sure that he had come out of this particularly well, but Alice felt her heart overflowing with admiration and gratitude. Edward was wonderful. Edward was *wonderful*. And to think she used not to like him! She remembered this morning early, herself sitting on the park seat thinking dreadful thoughts; she remembered the mist, and Edward's odd bony face coming through it, all shining and beautiful now, as he made the dreadful thoughts go away.

Oh, Edward was *wonderful*.

At lunch time Flora, who did not know the things had been given back, found herself standing behind Alice in the queue. 'There's a funny smell

121

round here,' she said loudly to Leanne, who was on her other side. 'Can you smell a funny smell in front of me?'

'Oh, drop it!' said Leanne. 'It's got boring now.'

The news seeped round, that the tormenting of Alice Cousins was over. Rather shamefaced, Patsy and Claire began to make overtures of friendship. Alice felt quite giddy; this rapid change in her fortunes was almost too much to grasp. There was Edward taking all that trouble to help her, and Patsy and Claire wanting to be friends – did that mean she was really worth something, after all?

She would be happy with what she had, she decided. It wasn't as much as she had once, but she would make it do. She would forget about the things she had before, since there was no way she was ever going to get them back ... How could she forget about the baby, though, her Harry? Well, she couldn't, but she could keep it as just a warm little secret, couldn't she? A precious memory, separate from all the horribleness and trouble. The trouble part she *would* forget, and not think of it again. She would concentrate on pleasing Miss Churchwood, and being friends with Patsy and Claire.

And she would think about Edward, who was so kind, and had done this wonderful wonderful thing, just for her!

Edward ran through the park, and arrived at his house breathless and panting. 'Grandma?'

Grandma was in the sitting room, and she had been to the shop as promised. 'Here they are, your twenty-five pounds and twenty-five more cards ...

All right, don't snatch, don't snatch, they won't run away!' Oddly enough, she didn't seem to be in any great hurry to see what was in the cards.

Edward thrust the twenty-five pounds into his pocket, sat on the sofa, and began to scratch furiously. 'Nothing ... nothing ... nothing ... There's three twos on this one ... And here's three fives.'

'Well, that's a start.'

'Nothing ... nothing ... nothing ... nothing ... nothing, *nothing*.' For the first time, there was a dreadful doubt in Edward's mind. 'I've done half of them now, and hardly any money!'

'Edward ...' Grandma sounded ever so slightly nervous.

'What?'

'I've been meaning to say ... Look, the stars aren't *always* right.'

'Yes, they are!'

'Well – usually, but not always. You mustn't be too disappointed ...'

'They *are* always right, they have to be!'

'Well, let's hope ... Do the rest.'

'Nothing ... nothing ... Oh, *Grandma*!'

'Well ... ?'

'It's a thousand!' Edward breathed. 'I've won a *thousand pounds*!' Once again there were fireworks exploding in his head, and now he was hardly sitting on the sofa any more, but floating, it seemed, several feet above it. It had worked, the plan had worked! It wasn't just a dream any more, it was real!

Grandma was just as excited. 'Show me!'

Edward handed her the card. 'I'm rich, I'm rich!'

Grandma was silent.

'A *thousand pounds*!' Edward marvelled.

'Actually, not,' said Grandma, in a sad sort of voice.

'What do you mean?'

'A mistake. Look. Two thousands and one ten, I'm afraid. See? One big nought and two little ones, this last one's a ten.'

Edward was furious. 'They do it on purpose! It's a cheat, they're cheaters!'

'I shouldn't have encouraged you . . . Anyway, you've still got a few more tickets to scratch.'

The remaining tickets yielded one more prize of just one pound.

'I don't understand!' Edward wailed. 'The stars said this was a good day. I was supposed to win, and I haven't!'

'I shouldn't have encouraged you,' said Grandma miserably, once again.

'I wasted my money, I wasted it!'

'Oh, Edward, I'm sorry.'

Edward was counting his meagre winnings. 'Eight pounds,' he said bitterly. 'Twenty-five pounds to win eight, what a swindle!'

'I'm sorry. I shouldn't have encouraged you.'

'Don't keep saying that, you're getting on my nerves . . . *I* know, *I* know . . . !'

'What?'

'The stars could be right all the time! They *are* right, they have to be! I'm meant to get eight more tickets with this. You have to go up the shop now, and get me eight more tickets, Grandma!'

Grandma looked tired. 'All right, but you mustn't be too disappointed . . .'

Ten minutes later she was back, looking even more tired.

'Well?'

'Look. Here they are. I scratched them for you. In the shop. In case I needed to go back again.'

'*And*?'

'Nothing. I'm sorry, Edward. I shouldn't have encouraged you.'

Edward sat on the sofa, devastated by the loss of all his hopes. All day he had been so sure and now . . . He would never do scratch cards again! *Ever*!

Grandma sat opposite him, not meeting his eyes. 'It's your fault!' he accused her. 'You made me do it!'

'I know. I shouldn't have put the idea in your head.'

'You made me believe those rubbish stars!'

'They do work sometimes.'

'Yes, well don't give me advice ever again! I can do without your advice, all right? You can stay out of my life from now on. Dad was right about everything. I'm on Dad's side now!'

On the television there was a play about a baby, who was abandoned by its mother, who was too young to look after it. The tears rolled down Emily's cheeks as she watched – she couldn't hold them back. Emily's mother was crying as well, but only because the story was so sad. 'Just look at you two!' her father joked. 'Pair of running taps, we shall be flooded out!'

Emily cried harder. She sniffed and sobbed, her thin shoulders jerking inside the baggy T-shirt. 'Come on,' said her father uneasily, 'that's a bit over the top, isn't it?'

'You don't understand.'

'No, I don't. I don't understand why you're getting so worked up about a *story*. It's not as though it's true.'

Emily blew her nose, and looked at her father with tragic eyes. 'It *could* be true, though. I mean, something like that really could happen, couldn't it?'

'Well, yes, I suppose it could. But it hasn't, has it? Not to anyone we know.'

Emily covered her face with her arms, and sobbed again. She was going to have to tell them. She couldn't keep it to herself any longer, couldn't bear it all by herself any more, not knowing what had happened. She heard herself saying the words, and her voice sounded like somebody else's.

'It *is* true!'

There, it was out, she couldn't go back now, she could only go on. Frightened, she waited for her parents' response.

Her father was still mystified. 'You mean . . . to one of your friends?' Her mother said nothing; she had a sudden dreadful suspicion about what was coming.

'Not to one of my friends – to *me*.'

'Rubbish!' said her father.

'It's not rubbish, it's true, I had a baby. Two weeks ago. I had him all by myself, and I left him in the park.'

There was a terrible, stunned silence.

126

'You *what*?' said her father at last.

'I knew there was something. I knew there was something.' Her mother whispered the words over and over again. 'You looking so peaky and miserable. But how did you ever manage . . . ?'

Her father had lapsed into silence again; her mother went on struggling to speak. 'You said . . . It was a boy, then?'

'Yes . . . I knew what to do. I cut the cord and everything.'

'And he was all right? I mean . . .'

'He was beautiful. He was perfect. He cried when he came out. I wrapped him in a towel and he went to sleep.'

'Oh, *Emily*!'

Her father still said nothing; Emily could not bear to look at him. 'Anyway, now you know, and I've let you down and I suppose now you're going to hate me.'

Emily's mother put her arms round Emily and hugged her close. 'Don't be silly, we could never hate you.'

'Whatever I did?'

'Whatever you did,' said her mother, firmly.

' . . . Dad?' Emily hardly dared ask him, but she had to know.

Emily's father cleared his throat. 'Well, it's a bit of a shock.' He tried to smile. 'You're still my little girl, though.'

It was gone! The crushing weight that was her secret had lifted, instantly dissolved into the air. Mum and Dad still loved her, they still loved her!

But what about her baby . . . ?

Emily cried again. 'Somebody took him, only it

wasn't on the telly. And I don't know where he is. And I want him, I want my baby!'

Emily's mother rocked Emily, rocked her and rocked her, while she tried to think of the right thing to say. 'He'll be all right, you know. People don't take babies to harm them, they take them to love them, and look after them.'

'But he's mine!' Emily wept. 'I don't want somebody else to love him, *I* want to do it!'

It was not the right time to point out all the mistakes she had made; in any case, she probably knew them already. 'Of course you do,' her mother murmured soothingly. 'Of course you want your baby, of course you do!'

Her father stood up suddenly. 'How about a cup of tea? I'll put the kettle on, and then we'll all have a good think, all of us together, about the best way to go about finding my grandson!'

The beginning of the adventure

Through a long, tormented night, Edward's thoughts went round and round. All his hopes gone, *crash!* This morning he had been certain of riches. He had been *certain*, and now . . . nothing! The disappointment was just too much to bear.

He must get himself back to where he was this morning. He must get himself back and quickly.

How?

Well, his baby of course. His baby was good for a thousand pounds at least! Margaret and Bill had to pay. It wasn't right to take other people's babies and not pay, it wasn't fair!

The problem was, though, they went away, didn't they? Didn't Alice say they went away, and she didn't know where they were?

Anyway, they had to pay. It wasn't fair if they didn't, and especially now it was so important to him to have the money, and get back to being rich, like he had expected to be.

Alice Cousins probably knew where they were all the time, anyway she must have some idea. They must have said something, some time, that would be a clue. He would make Alice remember the clue, so he could go after Margaret and Bill and make them pay for his baby.

All right, suppose Alice really didn't know anything useful, what then?

Well, he would have to find them some other way. There must be a clue somewhere. In their house for instance, perhaps the clue would be there. Alice didn't say if they took all their things with them, but they might have left *something* behind ... And they might have left that window open, like before ... And he could get into the house, and find the clue, and go after Margaret and Bill to get the money for his baby. Because it was only fair.

Tomorrow. Tomorrow he would question Alice Cousins, and if that failed, he would break into Number 27, like before. Only this time, ha, ha, there would be nobody to catch him.

Why couldn't he get to sleep so tomorrow would hurry up and come?

Rebecca and Miranda were falling out. The trouble was that Rebecca liked associating in a group, as well as having a best friend; and since Rebecca was used to getting her own way absolutely, and Miranda was used to getting *her* own way absolutely, there was no room for compromise. Rebecca accused Miranda of being a silly jealous cow, and Miranda accused Rebecca of always wanting her own way. They backed off from one another, screaming insults across the expanding distance.

Lacking a best friend once more, Miranda's thoughts turned back to Alice. Everyone was being nice to Alice again now, so there would be no loss of status there ...

She made her move at lunch time, pushing in at the canteen, so she could be behind Alice in the queue. 'Hi,' Miranda said breezily, as though there had never been a rift between them.

'Hi!' said Alice faintly; little currents of excitement whirled in her head, mingling with the smell of cabbage and beef stew.

'Can I sit with you today?'

'If you like.' Alice gave Miranda a small shy smile, which brought the heavy face to life, but was no measure of the joy which threatened to burst out of her chest.

Across the hall, Edward ground his teeth with frustration. He had planned to catch up with Alice on the way home, where he could talk to her without Leanne and that lot seeing, and getting the wrong idea or pretending to. Only now it looked like he wouldn't be able to get her alone, because she was teaming up again with that arch-nuisance Miranda!

He would have to chance it anyway. He trailed the two of them down Almond Avenue. 'Alice!' he called.

She turned round, and so did Miranda. 'Go away, Edward, we don't want you.'

'I'm not speaking to you, I'm speaking to Alice. It's important!'

'Say it to both of us then.'

'Huh! No chance! Come on, Alice,' Edward begged.

'Tell him to get lost,' said Miranda.

Alice said nothing, looking at the ground. How could she be rude to Edward, after what he did for her? But how could she defy Miranda, who was now so miraculously her best friend again? It seemed as though they were pulling at her, one

131

on each side, trying to tear her in two. She couldn't please both of them, but how could she decide?

Weakly, feeling terrible about Edward, Alice allowed Miranda to steer her through her own front gate, making for the playhouse just as before. Mercifully, Miranda seemed to have no curiosity about whatever it was Edward wanted.

Fuming and muttering to himself, Edward decided to be at Alice's house next morning, early, and catch her the minute she came out. He couldn't wait till tomorrow to get on with his plans, though – tomorrow was too long to wait.

All right, he'd do the other bit of his plan – he'd break into the house next door and look for clues. No need to wait for after dark this time; he couldn't get caught, could he, if there was no one inside to catch him.

Of course, there was always the chance that someone might see him going through the front gate – but so what? He could ring the doorbell, couldn't he? And when no one answered – which they wouldn't of course, because there was no one living there now – he could walk openly round to the back, as though looking for Margaret and Bill in the garden. And no one would suspect him, why should they?

Ha, ha, now that *was* a clever idea! Lucky he had been born clever; it did help, in this life, to have brains.

One nasty thought struck him as he stood at the back door – what about Miranda? Could he be seen from the playhouse? No, no, there were some nice thick bushes in the way, now wasn't that lucky!

The back door was locked. So, unfortunately,

was the kitchen window he had almost climbed through the time before. Edward considered breaking the window, and getting in that way, but found he wasn't quite brave enough. Well, all right, all right, that wasn't not being brave, that was just not being stupid.

There was another window, he found, that *was* open, just a crack, and that was at the side of the house, behind the garage. The trouble was, it did look very small. The glass was the thick bubbly kind, the sort you can't see through; it was only when Edward stood on tiptoe and reached to pull the casement fully out, that he realised he was looking into a downstairs lavatory.

The opening was *very* small – could he, somehow, squeeze through? Well, now, he wasn't fat, and that was one good thing. Gripping the inside sill, and hauling himself up by his arms, he stuck his head into the little space.

His shoulders were the problem. Edward twisted himself this way and that, and discovered that the only way he could get his shoulders through the little space was to position them diagonally across the opening. He wriggled some more. It was all very painful; Edward found his arms pressed excruciatingly against sharp corners, his knees being scraped over rough masonry. He hadn't expected all this pain; really, in a way, he would like to give up.

But no, no, he must go on – how else was he going to get back to feeling himself a rich man?

More painful jerks and wriggles then, and Edward found himself catapulted head first into the little lavatory. He managed to break his fall by grabbing at the edge of a wash basin as he slithered over it, but his forehead struck the lavatory pan, before hitting cold, hard linoleum.

Awkwardly, Edward eased the rest of himself to the floor, and clambered to his feet. He felt dizzy, and thought there was probably a bruise which would need some explaining. Never mind, first things first – his clue, concentrate on his clue!

Into the squiggly hall, and through to the squiggly sitting room. No clues here, as far as he could tell . . . Come to think of it, what would a clue actually *look* like? Never mind, he would surely recognise one if he saw it.

Nothing in the squiggly dining room, and nothing in the squiggly red and blue kitchen. Edward went up the squiggly stairs. There were a few clothes still hanging in the wardrobe of the front bedroom, and more in the chest of drawers – shabby things, though, old ones Margaret and Bill probably didn't want any more. Anyway, no clues.

A car drawing up outside attracted Edward's attention to the window. He stood against the wall and peered cautiously round the curtain. Getting out of the car were two people – a small, thin, disagreeable looking lady, and a big fat pleasant-faced man. Oh, *no*! They were coming up the path! Edward drew back and listened for the bell.

Nothing.

He tiptoed to the landing and listened again. Oh NO! There was the sound of a key being turned in the front door. The door was opening and they were coming *in*!

Margaret and Bill. It must be Margaret and Bill come back!

Edward was trapped.

He needed somewhere to hide. Where could he hide, where, where? On the landing was an airing cupboard, but that was still almost full. He went into the spare bedroom, and tried to get under the bed, but there was no room. He heard the back door being opened; what was happening now? He peeped out of the window – oh, joy, oh joy! The fat man and the thin lady were going into the garden! His feet on wings, Edward made for the stairs.

The thin lady, coming back into the hall, caught him halfway down. 'Who are you?' Her voice was sharp and sour and matched her face.

Edward tried to make a rush for it, then suddenly stopped.

After all, why worry?

What did it matter if he was caught? He wanted to speak to Margaret and Bill anyway, that was what all this was about! Ha, ha, he nearly boobed there, getting in a panic all for nothing. 'I'm the one that found the baby,' he said with new-found confidence.

'What baby?'

'You know – *the* baby!'

The big fat man appeared. 'Hullo, what have we got here?'

'Some kid broke in, by the looks of it. Says he found a baby.'

'Not *a* baby,' said Edward, '*the* baby.'

'I don't know anything about a baby,' said the man.

'Yes you do. I know you've got it because I saw the bottle. And anyway, Alice told me, so you can't get out of it.'

'He's barking!' said the lady.

'No I'm not! It was my baby, and I don't mind if you have it, but you have to pay. A thousand pounds.'

The big man began to laugh.

'All right,' Edward conceded, 'five hundred. In cash, of course.'

'Don't you think we should get the police?' said the lady.

'You can't do that!' said Edward, triumphantly. 'If you do that we might *all* end up in prison. Because of the baby. Because we didn't take it to the hospital.'

'I think we should get the police,' said the lady.

'*No!*' Edward was alarmed now. 'Didn't you understand about going to prison?'

'I haven't understood a word you've said so far,' said the fat man.

'I don't know why we don't just get the police,' said the lady. 'Then I can get on with viewing the house.'

A great doubt hit Edward like a thunderbolt. In his mind's eye there was a picture of the FOR SALE notice outside. BARNES and BRADCOME, the notice said. Was the fat man from BARNES and BRADCOME then? And the lady . . . ? 'Aren't you Margaret and Bill, then?'

'Who are they?'

Edward gulped. 'Sorry, I made a mistake. I'll just go.'

'I wouldn't let him if I were you,' said Sour-face. 'He's probably stolen something.'

Edward lunged for the front door. The fat man barred his way. Edward turned, to run through the kitchen, into the back garden and down the garden path. It was madness what he was doing, he knew that. There would be no way out at the bottom of the garden, but what choice did he have? To go round the side of the house would be to run into the arms of the fat man and the thin lady . . .

Miranda glanced out of the playhouse window. 'Oh, look! There's Edward Lawson again!'

'Where?' said Alice, faintly.

'Running down the garden next door. There's two people running after him, as well. Let's go and see!' Grinning, Miranda hurried outside, and stood peering through the fence. Alice followed slowly, her heart beginning to thump. What was Edward doing next door, as though she couldn't guess! Now Miranda *was* going to get curious. There could be awkward questions; things could get dragged out that were best buried and forgotten.

'Hullo, Edward,' Miranda called, 'fancy seeing you here!'

Edward stopped running, because there was no longer anywhere to go. 'Do you know this character?' said Sour-face to Miranda.

'Oh, yes. We know him ever so well, don't we, Alice?'

'Does he make a habit of breaking into houses?'

'I expect so.' Miranda was delighted. Now *that*

would be something to spread round the class tomorrow; she could hardly wait.

'I didn't steal anything,' Edward pleaded. 'I didn't, I didn't!'

'Some tarradiddle about finding a baby,' said the fat man, 'that I had to pay for. He seemed to think I was somebody called Bill. Mean anything to you?'

Swallowing her excitement, Miranda shook her head. 'It's his imagination. He's always imagining things, isn't he, Alice? He's a bit loopy, actually.'

Sour-face snorted. 'I'd say that's an under-statement!'

'Oh, look,' said Edward desperately, 'there's a UFO!'

All except Miranda raised their eyes to the sky; Edward dodged and ran. It worked, it worked! Edward's self-esteem, trailing on the ground a moment before, came surging up as he went. I'm a clever person after all, he reassured himself. They can't get the better of *me*, none of them!

Miranda watched regretfully, as Edward legged it up the garden path. 'What a pity you fell for that old trick!'

The fat man muttered something; the sour-faced lady was already retreating towards the house. Grinning again, Miranda turned to Alice. 'That was the best thing that happened all day, actually. Don't you think that was the best thing?'

'I suppose so.'

'Silly Edward!' said Miranda. 'He could get us all in trouble, telling people about the baby like that! Good thing I thought of saying he imagined it ... I don't really believe we'd go to prison though. You don't *really* believe that, do you, Alice? . . . Anyway, now we have a mystery to solve.'

'Have we?'

'Of course. About the baby, what Edward *said* about the baby, didn't you hear? I've got a theory already. Part of one, at least.'

'Have you?' said Alice, unhappily.

'Yes . . . You know that night when the baby got stolen?'

'Yes.'

'Well,' said Miranda triumphantly, 'I think it was Edward stole it!'

'Edward wouldn't have done that.'

'How do you know?'

'Edward doesn't steal. Anyway, why would he when he just then left it for us to look after?'

'There might be a reason . . . Why are you standing up for horrible Edward?'

'I'm not . . . Let's play something!'

'I don't want to play something, I want to talk about the mystery. Why don't you want to talk about the mystery?'

Alice floundered. 'I don't know. It's boring . . . Let's do some handstands, I can nearly do handstands now, look!'

Miranda stood, thoughtfully watching Alice's clumsy efforts. 'I think there's something you're not telling me. Something about the baby.'

'No there isn't.'

'Seems like it's got something to do with next door . . . Why are Margaret and Bill selling their house?'

'I don't know . . . I'm sorry.'

'Have *they* got the baby? They have, haven't they?

They've got the baby and they went away with it, didn't they? Why didn't you tell me?'

'I couldn't,' Alice whispered. 'They made me promise.'

'But you could have told *me.*'

Alice was silent. Why couldn't she be allowed to forget all that, like she wanted to? Of course, in a way, it would be a relief to spill it all out to Miranda, and not have any more secrets. But would Miranda ever forgive her for the great big lie she told in the first place?

'I tell you what,' Miranda offered. 'I'll let you off not telling me before if you tell me everything now. *Everything*!'

Alice could not speak. Her throat felt tight, closed up, almost, her head about to burst. 'If you don't tell me,' Miranda urged, 'you can't be my best friend.'

Alice took a deep breath. 'All right . . . But after I told you, can we just forget it, and never talk about it again?'

Two fine days, and the clouds were back – black ones this time, hanging low in the sky. Early in the morning, Edward waited outside Alice's house. Come on, Alice, come on! Come on before the rain starts. Hurry up and come so I can find out if you know anything useful!

Edward glared impatiently at Alice's front door. What was she doing? Why was she taking all this time in there, when he needed her out here? Behind him, unseen, Miranda approached, and shouted in his ear. 'BOO!'

'Get lost!'

'Excuse me, I'm calling for Alice.'

Edward ground his teeth with rage. 'And I want to speak to Alice privately. Why don't you just drop dead?'

'Why don't you emigrate, or something? You wanted to sell the dear, darling, lovely little baby, didn't you? See? I know all about that, Alice told me!'

'It was mine. I found it, I can do what I like with it, all right?'

Miranda laughed. 'How can you do what you like with it, when Margaret and Bill took it away?'

Edward ignored her. He swung on the Cousins' gate while Miranda went to ring the bell. In the doorway, Alice hid her dismay at seeing Edward. Now she was going to have to choose between them like yesterday, and have all that old stuff dragged up *again*. Whatever it was Edward wanted, she realised, it was bound to be something to do with Harry. Alice's heart went thump, thump, thump, as wooden-faced, arm in arm with Miranda, she trudged stolidly through the gate. Edward positioned himself on her other side, and the three of them started walking together.

'Look, you have to help me, Alice,' Edward said. 'You have to think where Margaret and Bill have gone. Because they have to pay me for the baby, it's only fair!'

'Alice doesn't want to talk about that,' said Miranda. 'She wants to forget all about it.'

'I wasn't speaking to you!'

'I'm only standing up for my best friend.'

'She doesn't need you to stand up for her. Come on, Alice, *think*!'

141

Alice didn't want to have to think, she wanted Edward to go away. But she must do what he asked, mustn't she, after what he did for her? Only please, *please*, don't let it offend Miranda too much! 'I don't know anything for certain,' she said.

'All right, all right, do you know anything for *un*certain?'

'Well, I did think, when they went away first, they might have gone to their caravan . . . I don't know, though, they might have gone anywhere.'

Edward felt his heart leap with joy and excitement. 'They have got a caravan, though, you do know that!'

'Yes . . . I saw some pictures of it once. It's by the seaside.'

'Well that's it, that's where they went for certain . . . Which seaside?'

'I don't know. I forget.'

'Well remember! Remember, Alice, you can if you want to!'

'Leave her alone,' said Miranda.

'I'm not hurting her.'

'Yes you are, you're bullying her! Stop bullying my best friend!'

'Who asked you to stick your nose in?'

'I think it's Clappingdean,' said Alice. 'I don't know for sure, though . . . My mum might know.'

'Ask her this evening!' Edward demanded. 'Go on, Alice, you ask your mum this evening, all right?'

'She doesn't have to if she doesn't want to,' said Miranda.

'Shut your face!'

142

The rain came then, hard and heavy, and they all began to run.

Emily had gone to the police station with her mother and father. The policewoman was very kind, very patient with Emily when she cried. 'Just tell me everything you can remember. Take your time.'

'I left him in the park.'

'Where in the park, exactly?'

Emily was about to say: 'Under a seat near the gate,' but was suddenly stricken with shame. She couldn't bring herself to admit she put her baby *under* the seat. It was bad enough having to tell her story at all – people didn't need to know quite how wicked she had been, did they?

'I put him on a seat,' she said. 'Near the gate.'

10

Making plans

Edward gave up trying to concentrate on his work. If Miss Churchwood wanted to know why he hadn't done any, he would have to say he had a headache. From the way his thoughts were zooming around he soon would have a headache anyway. Buzz, buzz, zoom, zoom – already he felt quite faint and giddy.

Clappingdean. Clap, clap, clappety clap! It sounded like a train, didn't it – and that was how he would get there, by train. He knew the station and everything, so it would be easy peasy. What a lucky thing that he and Grandma had gone to that very seaside one day, in half term.

There was one small problem, and that was the matter of the ticket. Of course, he had his savings, but they were for being a millionaire, not for wasting on train tickets. He would just have to hide from the ticket man; Edward practised doing it in his mind, and that was easy peasy as well.

So what would the next thing be?

Well – first find the caravans; when he went with Grandma, that other time, they had just made their way through the town until they found the beach. He hadn't seen any caravans, they must be somewhere else, but someone would be able to tell him where they were. Then walk around till he found Margaret and Bill. Not quite easy peasy

– Edward had never seen Margaret and Bill, he had no idea what they looked like. Remember yesterday, and the embarrassing mistake he made then!

All right, all right, he would have to ask some more. He would have to ask where Margaret and Bill's caravan was, and if they were out, just hang around till they came back . . .

Wouldn't that look funny, though? Might not people get suspicious, and start asking *him* questions . . . ? And supposing he couldn't find anyone who knew Margaret and Bill by name . . . ?

There was one other teeny weeny problem as well – Margaret and Bill didn't know *him*. Supposing they didn't believe him when he said he was the one that found the baby . . . ?

Now, it was just an idea but supposing . . . ?

Oh, no, he didn't want that, he really would rather not! She was only good for looking after babies, and not much good at that. She'd get in the way, mostly, and be all sorts of trouble.

It would solve a lot of the problems, though, wouldn't it, if he did his idea!

Once more, in the morning, Edward waited outside Alice's house. He swung on her gate, and brooded darkly. Let Miranda have broken her leg, let her have the mumps; what a pity her house hasn't burned down, in the night! And here she comes, Number One pest, smirking and grinning and thinking herself *it*.

'You again!' said Miranda.

'I suppose it's too much to ask, if I want to speak to Alice without your lugs flapping!'

145

'You're right, it is too much to ask.'

Miranda called for Alice, while Edward fumed and scowled. He followed close behind, trying to speak into Alice's ear. 'Did you ask your mum?'

'She says it's Clappingdean. She thinks.'

'Are you going there, then, Edward?' said Miranda. 'To look for them? If you are, you're mad!'

Edward whispered something to Alice, his chin almost on her shoulder. 'Oh, no!' Alice cried in dismay. 'Oh, no, I couldn't! I'm sorry.'

'What does he want you to do now?' said Miranda.

'He wants me to go to Clappingdean with him.'

'That's right,' said Edward, bitterly. 'Tell everyone!'

Miranda shrieked with laughter. 'You're bonkers, Edward!'

'Please don't ask me to do it!' Alice begged. 'Please don't ask me to go with you, Edward!'

'Well, I wouldn't, only I think it might go wrong if you don't come.'

'Yes, but—'

'It's to make it fair, Alice. They might not believe me if you don't tell them. And anyway, you have to show me which is them, to make sure I have the right ones.'

'But you'd both get in trouble!' Miranda squealed. 'Haven't you thought your parents will wonder where you've gone?'

'You don't know anything, Miranda! We won't get in trouble, because we'll be there and back before half past three. Our parents will think we're in school.'

'Oh . . . Miss Churchwood won't think you're in school, though.'

'She'll think we're ill. Or we had to go to the dentist or something.'

'What about the next day – when you haven't got any notes to bring?'

'Don't make difficulties . . . I know, we can say we lost them.'

'Oh.' Miranda looked thoughtful. 'Anyway, it will cost a lot of money to go all that way.'

'No it won't, it won't cost any money at all! We can go by train, and hide from the ticket man, all right?

' . . . Oh.'

'And it will be a lot of fun!'

' . . . *Oh*,' said Miranda.

Alice sat miserably in school, her mind in turmoil. Was it really Edward's baby, like he said? He *had* found it, of course, but did that really give him the right to sell it? It wasn't Margaret's, that was certain, Margaret and Bill just stole it, so perhaps they ought to pay, like Edward said . . . But was the baby really *Edward's*? For a long time she had thought the baby was hers; she had *felt* Harry was hers because she loved him so much . . . But whose baby was he really?

One thing *was* clear – she owed Edward a good turn because of the wonderful thing he did for her. Was Edward himself really as wonderful as she had thought him? Alice wasn't too sure about that any more, but she was sure about owing him a good turn. Only this was too much to ask, wasn't it? Too much!

At playtime, Miranda was preoccupied. She scuffed restlessly at the ground with her toe, and the corners of her mouth quivered in an excited little smile. At last she spoke. 'You know what Edward said, this morning . . .'

'It *is* a mad idea, isn't it?' said Alice, anxiously.

'Yes, but . . . it *would* be fun, you know, it would be an adventure!'

'Do you agree with Edward now, then? That Margaret and Bill have to pay? Because it was really Edward's baby?'

'What? Oh, that! Yes, I suppose so.'

'I know – why don't you go instead of me?'

'Oh, not *instead* of you, Alice, *with* you!'

'I don't want to, though. It's not sensible.'

'Oh, you're not going on about being *sensible* again, are you? Don't you want to see the dear darling lovely little baby? Perhaps Margaret will let us hold him, don't you want to hold the baby again?'

Of course Alice wanted to see Harry again. To hold him, and love him like before . . . But what about the danger? Fear and longing pulled opposite ways inside her, and fear won. 'I don't want to get in trouble,' she whispered.

'Well you won't, will you, how can you get in trouble? Come on, Alice, let's do it, eh? Eh? Please pretty please with sugar on top, say yes!'

Edward caught up with them on the way home. 'How about it, then?' he said to Alice. 'Are you coming?'

'I haven't decided.'

'Yes, you have!' Miranda protested. 'You *did*

decide! We decided it together at playtime. We're both coming!'

Edward almost exploded. '*You?* I didn't ask you, I only asked Alice!'

'Well bad luck, because Alice won't come without me, will you, Alice?'

Alice felt weak. Her knees wobbled, and her insides seemed about to fall out. Why did this have to happen? Just when everything was good again, just when she was happy, this great dark monster had to drop out of the sky. This creature with the huge black wings had to fall on her, and smother her, so she could hardly breathe for fear of what the monster was forcing her to do.

I don't want to, she wailed silently. I don't want to! Even for the chance of seeing Harry again, it's too frightening. I don't want to do it!

But how could she refuse?

It would have to be Monday, Edward said. But then Miranda insisted Tuesday would be better, because she had a great idea for how to stop Miss Churchwood being even the tiniest bit suspicious, when none of them turned up for school. Edward fumed and protested – and angrily gave in. If Miranda didn't get her way, she might not come. And if Miranda didn't come, then Alice wouldn't come either, probably. He could have a wasted journey, and perhaps trouble as well.

Alice spent a wretched weekend.

She had agreed to go, because with both of them at her she couldn't *not* agree. But it surely must be wrong, and Mum and Dad would be dreadfully unpleased with her if they found out.

Edward said they *wouldn't* find out, and Miranda seemed to believe that, and she wanted to believe it herself, and of course Edward had been to Clappingdean before, so he would know how long it took, wouldn't he?

But then, would Margaret and Bill really be at the caravan? Edward believed it, but then he *wanted* to believe it, didn't he? He wanted to believe it so much he wouldn't hear of any other possibility. He was sure they'd pay up when they were asked, as well. And perhaps he was right . . .

Harry!

She would be seeing Harry again!

For a moment, that bright and lovely thought shone through the murky tumult in her mind. Harry! She ached to see him, she really did. Perhaps it would be worth going just for that . . .

And once more the question with no answer to it – whose baby was he really?

Utterly confused, Alice struggled through Saturday and Sunday. The weather was horrible – rain, rain, rain. Miranda was tied up with her family – visiting her grandparents on Saturday, and with a houseful of cousins arriving on Sunday. So Alice brooded in the playhouse all by herself, her thoughts as dark as the sky outside, wishing that things could be as they were, before any of these troubles started.

She didn't imagine what going to Clappingdean would be like, or what might happen once they got there, because she couldn't. Every time the thought came she could see only a thick grey wall, hiding formless and unspeakable disasters. Her mind bounced off the wall, to flounder in a heaving sea of dread.

On Monday it was still raining. 'If it's like this tomorrow it won't be much of a day for going to the seaside,' Miranda complained. She was bubbling with excitement, though, giggling and throwing herself about and generally creating a centre of fuss. Miss Churchwood's going to think something's up, Edward thought fiercely. Egg-brain Miranda's going to give it away, and that's *before* we have to do this stupid idea she's dreamed up!

In his heart, he had to admit that Miranda's idea might not be all that stupid. Three of them away tomorrow might indeed look suspicious. It might even involve phone calls to their homes or something – teachers were well known for being awkward busybodies!

Miranda mustn't overdo it, though. Edward groaned inwardly as he imagined the drama, the mooing voice, the rolling eyes. He'd warned her about that, and she'd claimed to understand; they mustn't be ill enough to have the welfare assistant sent for, their parents phoned, everything spoiled!

He need not have worried; Miranda did her bit all right. Twenty minutes before home time, as planned, she put up her hand and said, with quite a convincing choke in her voice: 'Please Miss Churchwood, I feel sick!'

'Go on, then.'

Miranda stumbled out of the classroom, one hand clamped firmly to her mouth. Five minutes later she was back, looking woebegone, but not too woebegone. 'All right?' said Miss Churchwood.

'Yes thank you. I've just got a bit of a headache.'

'Sit quietly, then. We'll see how you are at home time.'

Ten minutes later, Edward ran for the door. 'Where are you going, Edward?'

'I feel sick!'

'Oh dear, another one!' said Miss Churchwood.

Edward returned. 'Well?'

'I'm all right, I wasn't *actually* sick.'

The bell rang. 'Are you all right for going home, Miranda?' said Miss Churchwood.

'Oh yes, I feel much better now.'

'Anyway, Alice will be going with you, won't you, Alice?'

'Yes.' Miranda gave her a little nudge. 'Actually I've got a *little* bit of headache myself. Not very much,' she added, quickly.

'I hope there isn't some bug going round,' said Miss Churchwood.

Edward and Grandma sat side by side on the sofa. They were not speaking; since that unfortunate episode with the scratch cards, Edward and his grandma had exchanged only a few formal words, now and again. Edward could not avoid seeing, out of the corner of his eye, the hurt and sadness in Grandma's face, but he hardened his heart and pretended he couldn't. Or that he didn't care anyway.

Dad, in the armchair, his eyes glued to the television news, did not seem to have noticed that Edward and Grandma were not speaking.

The main news finished, and now it was time for the local news. Suddenly Edward's eyes also were riveted on the screen. *What* was he saying? What was the television announcer saying? A baby? Left in Edge Hill Park? Three weeks ago? On a seat near the gate! *And now his real mother wants him back.*

Does she now! Well, she shouldn't have thrown him away in the first place, should she?

Anyway, the man said *on* the seat, didn't he? I distinctly heard him say it – *on* the seat, he said, and my baby was *under* the seat. So it must be a different baby.

Probably lots of babies get left in Edge Hill Park, people are always throwing their babies away.

It's not my baby they're talking about on the television, it's another one.

It *is*!

11

Some narrow escapes

'Did you bring your swimming costume?' Miranda asked Alice.

Edward snorted. 'What d'you want swimming costumes for?'

'To wrap round our necks of course,' said Miranda, with heavy sarcasm. 'In case it gets cold.'

'We aren't going to Clappingdean for swimming, you silly mad cow. We're going to find Margaret and Bill.'

'Oh, *that*! Well afterwards we can go swimming, can't we – you wonderful, clever, madly intelligent genius!'

The children were hiding in the park. Edward said they should leave, apparently for school, very early – wearing their uniforms, of course. They must get to the park before anyone from school saw them, and hide there until it was safe to come out and make for the station – Edge Hill Station, from where they would get an Underground train to Victoria, Edward said. Deep inside him there was beginning to be a ripple, just the tiniest ripple, of doubt about the timing of this adventure. Were they really going to be able to get to Clappingdean and back before half past three, like he'd promised? But they couldn't risk starting any earlier. Edward comforted himself with reminders of how long a day was, in school. Hours and hours and hours – sometimes it seemed the day would never end, of *course* there would be enough time.

There was another source of unease, so small and so far back in Edward's mind that it didn't even amount to a ripple. He didn't try to identify it; some things were best disregarded . . .

'Anyway, it looks like nice weather after all,' said Miranda hopefully, as a watery sun broke through the clouds.

Alice had not brought her swimming costume. In her school bag was her homework from yesterday, in case Mum should notice she had left it behind; half a packet of stale biscuits which Alice didn't think would be missed; two bananas taken from a very large bunch; and three pounds forty-five pence, which was the sum total of her savings at that time. The money had been intended for a present for Dad's birthday, but now it might be needed for emergencies.

Besides her swimming costume, Miranda had a small towel, a comb, and one pound for an ice cream – because no one ever heard of going to the seaside and not having an ice cream, did they?

Edward had brought nothing, because his bag needed to be empty for carrying all the money he was going to be bringing back. He had brought no money of his own; what would he need money for? His money was safest left at home.

'Nine o'clock!' said Miranda, who was the only one with a watch.

The Underground station was not far. There was no one in the booking office, and no one to ask them why they hadn't got a ticket. There was a machine, for buying tickets, and a rather ominous notice to the effect that if you were caught travelling without one, you would be fined ten pounds on the spot.

'If we see the inspector, we have to get off the train and run,' Edward explained.

'Have you done this before?' said Miranda.

'No, I just worked it out in my head. It helps to have brains, you know!'

'Listen to him, Alice. Anybody'd think he was the only person in the world that ever had good ideas.'

'You both have good ideas,' said Alice, desperate to keep the peace.

They sat in a row, waiting for the train. 'Oh, no!' Miranda exclaimed. 'Just look who's coming!'

'*Keith*!' Edward's heart sank. He could spit! He could spit, he could say bad words, he could punch Keith's silly face in. Perhaps Keith wouldn't see them; he was half blind after all!

Keith blinked, behind his thick glasses. There was a slow smile of recognition. 'Hullo!'

'Where're you going?'

'To the eye hospital. For my eyes.'

'That's funny,' said Miranda. 'We're going to the hospital too.'

'Oh . . . Are you?'

'Not the same hospital. A different one. For our headaches . . . You remember; yesterday we all had a headache, and Miss Churchwood said it must be something going round.'

'Oh . . . Yeah.'

'So we have to go to the hospital for it.'

Keith peered around. 'Who's taking you, then?'

'Nobody. We're going by ourself, like you.'

'Oh . . . Yeah . . . I'm not going by myself, though. My mum's just getting the tickets, from the machine.'

Miranda swallowed. 'I don't mean *just* by ourself, of course I don't mean that! I mean Alice and I are going without our mums, because Edward's grandma is very kindly taking all of us.'

Nice one, Miranda! Half grateful, half resentful, Edward kicked himself mentally for not being quick enough to think of all that for himself. 'She's getting tickets from the machine as well,' he contributed. 'There she is, just coming down the steps! Yoo-hoo, Grandma!'

He waved, and Miranda waved; and belatedly, guiltily aware that the others could see her not waving, Alice waved too.

'She can't see us. Here we are, Grandma!' Edward, Alice and Miranda leaped to their feet and charged for the steps so they wouldn't have to talk to Keith any more. The train came as they were running, and they piled in – far enough along the platform now to be in a different carriage from Keith.

The train rocked and swayed along the track. 'I'm enjoying this,' said Miranda. 'Aren't you enjoying it, Alice?'

'Yes,' said Alice, miserably.

Only a few hours and it will all be over, she tried to tell herself. I just have to bear it, and get through it, and trust Edward that we will be home before our parents can find out what we did.

They were not in the tunnels yet. This stretch of the track was open to the sky, with banks of tangled bushes on either side, and people's back gardens beyond. Miranda twisted round to peer hopefully upward. 'I can see blue sky!' she announced. 'I can see a little patch of blue sky, can't you, Alice?'

'Yes,' said Alice.

'It's getting bigger. The blue sky is getting bigger, isn't it, Alice!'

'It is getting bigger.'

'It's *really* big now!'

If she goes on about the blue sky much more, Edward thought, I shall probably hit her.

'It's getting hot,' said Miranda. 'Don't you think it's getting hot, Alice? I do, I think it's getting *boiling*! Phew! It's too hot to wear my coat!' She took it off, and put it on the empty seat beside her, wearing just her school uniform now – a thin green cardigan over a distinctive blue, green and white checked cotton dress. 'What a long way before we go under the ground! When are we going to get to that bit, Edward?'

'What time is it?' He hated having to ask her. When he got his money from Margaret and Bill he would buy himself a watch, Edward promised himself. There would be plenty left over for being a millionaire.

'Just gone half past nine,' said Miranda.

That was all right, that wasn't too bad; they would be in the tunnels soon, then they must look out for Oxford Circus, because that was where they had to change trains . . .

Darkness suddenly, as the train plunged under-ground. Edward fixed his eyes on the map above the seats, and began to count the stations.

'The ticket man's coming,' said Alice, in a small flat voice.

Edward shot to his feet, grabbing at the nearest pole to save himself from being toppled over by the swaying of the train. 'Get to the door!' There were several other people standing near the door. Alice found herself hemmed in by a large body, and knew a moment of panic as she fought her way round it to be with the others. 'Come on, station, *come on station*,' Edward implored, out loud. Miranda giggled.

The inspector was working his way remorselessly down the carriage. Two more seats, and he would have reached the children.

One more seat.

The inspector was requesting to see the ticket of the large body behind Alice. They were going to get caught – there was no escape! Alice began to calculate wildly; there wasn't enough money in her bag for *one* ten pound fine, let alone three!

A glimmer of light. The light getting brighter. The train slowing, slowing, the station rushing into view. PADDINGTON, said the lettering along the wall. But the doors were still closed, they couldn't get out.

'Girlie?' said the inspector, to Alice.

Alice reached into her bag. Perhaps if she said that was all she had, the inspector would accept one pound for each of them, instead of ten. Perhaps the fine was less for children, anyway. But then everything happened at once. The doors slid open, and Alice felt Edward gripping her arm. He yanked her on to the platform, with Miranda somehow on the other side, and the three of them ran, bumping into people as they went. They turned into the first exit they came to, and stood at a safe distance, watching the train they had left beginning to move out of the station. They watched it gather speed, and disappear from sight, carrying the ticket inspector with it. 'That was fun,' said Miranda.

Edward had enjoyed it too, and would have enjoyed it more if it were not for the ripple of doubt still there, at the back of his mind. 'We wasted some time,' he said. 'Now we have to wait for the next train.'

'I hope there's another inspector,' Miranda declared. 'I really enjoyed running away from that one . . . Oh, dear!'

Alice had only just finished getting her breath back; now Miranda's fallen face filled her with new apprehension. 'What's the matter?'

'I left my coat on the train.'

Edward snorted. 'Serve you right! Making out it's so hot when it isn't! Just because you want to go swimming.'

'What am I going to tell my mum, though?'

She was subdued all the way to Oxford Circus, where they had to change on to the Victoria line, as Edward remembered from before.

At Victoria there was a difficulty – the barriers! Edward had forgotten the barriers; there were no barriers at Edge Hill Station, but now he saw them he remembered the ones at Victoria. You put your ticket in the slot, he remembered, and the barriers opened automatically. That was fine for him and Grandma; the trouble this time was, they had no tickets.

'We could crawl underneath, perhaps,' he suggested, though he could see at a glance that the space beneath was very low. Hands and knees would not do, you would have to lie full length and wriggle.

'Alice is too fat,' said Miranda, who seemed to have thrown off her concerns about the missing coat.

'Don't be so rude!' said Edward. 'Anyway, she isn't fat – not really. There's girls in our class a lot fatter than Alice – Flora, for instance!'

Miranda shrugged. 'Alice doesn't mind me saying she's fat, do you, Alice?'

Alice did mind. She was hurt by Miranda's tactlessness, and even more upset by Edward's suggestion. She imagined herself getting stuck, and having to be pulled out by that man in the dark blue uniform of the London Underground, at the end of the row. And what would happen after that was too terrifying even to consider.

They must plan it carefully, and go one by one, Edward said – but Miranda was already face down on the ground, her bag thrown over the barrier, her slim agile body snaking its way through. No one tried to stop her; no one even seemed to notice, though there were plenty of other passengers using the barriers.

In a few moments she was standing on the other side, waving her bag and grinning. Nice one, Miranda, oh *nice* one! 'You next, Alice,' said Edward, hopefully. As usual, Alice's face showed little of what she was feeling inside, but Edward, standing beside her, was uncomfortably aware of her rapid breathing. 'Go on,' he encouraged her.

'In that empty one – now! You'll be all right, you saw how Miranda did it!'

Alice stumbled obediently forward, threw her bag over, dropped first to her knees and then her round stomach. Apart from anything else she felt silly. She must look *extremely* silly, she thought, a tubby thing like her trying to do the same things thin people could do. She tried to wriggle, but somehow her bottom would only go up and down, not from side to side like Miranda's. She felt something scraping the back of her head and, in a panic, pressed her face harder against the floor.

There was a voice behind her: 'Hey! What's going on?' But the voice was amused rather than angry. Watching anxiously, Edward saw how the large passenger behind her was hiding Alice's sticky progress through the barrier. In particular, he was hiding Alice from the eyes of the man in uniform – eyes which at that moment were apparently focused right at the barrier in question.

'Go on!' Alice heard the voice behind encouraging her. 'You've nearly made it, nearly! Well done!' Alice felt Miranda's hands grabbing her under the arms and hauling the rest of her through.

It was over! By some miracle this particularly nasty bit of the adventure was over!

Edward felt his spirits soar.

Now it was his turn he would be really cunning, really clever, he decided. Ha, ha, he would work it so that he was shielded from view like Alice had been – not by accident in his case, but because of the brilliance of his plan. He positioned himself by an empty barrier, and pretended to be

162

searching for his ticket, keeping a crafty eye on the man in uniform while he did so.

Someone was talking to the man in uniform; now let a passenger come to this barrier! Come on, come on, come on!

Now!

Edward pushed in front of the approaching woman, and threw himself happily on the ground. This was great! This was living! He hadn't bothered to throw his bag; his empty bag was no hindrance.

'Stop that, you little monkey!'

Edward's joy turned to aggrieved dismay. What was the matter with this unsporting person? She was supposed to laugh, and take it all in good part, not be annoyed with him! Anxiously now, Edward squeezed through the barrier and scrambled to his feet. The girls, he could see, were waiting for him a little way off.

But, would you believe it, the old misery had actually grassed him up! She had gone to the man in uniform and was pointing with her finger, right to where he stood!

And the man in uniform was coming!

Edward ran.

'Look at Edward running!' said Miranda with satisfaction, to Alice. There was no need for them to run, there was nothing at that point to link them with the fleeing Edward.

'We've lost him!' said Alice. Nightmare, again. One nightmare after another – worse than she had anticipated, even. 'Where do you think he's gone?'

'Find somewhere to hide, I suppose.'

'What are we going to do?' Alice's voice had shrunk to a whisper.

'I dunno . . . Go in the main line station and see if he's there? *I* dunno.' Miranda didn't sound particularly concerned.

'Do you think he's all right?'

Miranda linked arms with Alice and steered her, in a slow stroll, along the passageway. 'You don't want to bother about *him* . . . I know, why don't us two go to Clappingdean ourselves?'

Alice was dismayed. 'We can't leave Edward, though!' Not Edward, who had stopped her having dreadful thoughts, and saved an impossible situation by getting her things back for her!

Miranda went on as though Alice had not spoken. 'I don't know why I didn't think of it before; we don't really need him.'

'But we do! We need him to show us how to find the right train! And . . . all sorts of things.'

Miranda shrugged, and remembered how far this proposed journey was. Of *course* she couldn't go with just Alice, whatever was she thinking about! If she went with just Alice she would have to be the leader of the adventure and, well, it had to be admitted she didn't quite have the confidence for that. 'All right,' Miranda conceded. 'Don't worry, we're going with your precious Edward.'

They reached the main line station and stood in the middle of a great empty space, unsure what to do next.

'There's Edward!' said Alice, suddenly.

He was standing a vast distance away with his back to them, staring up at the departures board. Alice took a step forward, but Miranda yanked her back. 'Wait a minute, I want to go to the loo.'

'Won't there be one on the train?'

164

'I don't like the loos on trains. Loos on trains are horrid, and smelly. Anyway, I want to go *now*.'

'Shouldn't we tell Edward we're here, though?'

'Make him wait. Do him good.'

'He might be worried . . .'

'Oh, come *on*!'

They found the Ladies, after much searching, but it was twenty pence to go in. 'I haven't got any change,' Miranda said. 'Have you got any change, Alice?'

Alice had two twenty pence pieces.

'Oh good!' said Miranda. 'Enough for one each.'

'*I* don't want to go.'

'Oh please, Alice, please come in with me! Please pretty please with sugar on top!'

It was a waste of precious money, and Alice regretted the loss, but how could she say no to her best friend?

Afterwards, Miranda spent an interminable time fussing over her green and blue and white school dress, which had got dirty from wriggling on the ground. She sponged it and sighed over it, and when that was finished she had to comb her hair. Several different ways. 'Do you think it looks best like this, Alice . . . or like this?'

After something like eternity, Miranda consented to leave her hair, and go to find Edward. Edward was still by the departures board, and Edward was furious.

'Where have you been all this time? We've missed the train now!'

Miranda smiled and tossed her head, so the

newly combed hair bounced and shimmered. 'So? There'll be another one.'

But there wasn't – not for a long, long time. Edward and Miranda made insulting remarks to one another, and Alice could not have said how much she was hating this day. I want to go home, she cried inside herself.

And now the next bit is going to happen, Alice thought miserably. And the next bit is going to be worse than the first bit, because it's going to take me far away. It's going to take me far, far away!

And I'm starting to be afraid we won't get back in time, and Mum and Dad are going to find out what I did. I'm scared to try to work it out, but it seems like this first bit has taken a long long time already . . .

12

Stowaways

They sat in the stationary train – Alice and Miranda side by side, Edward by himself facing them. Now they were at last on their way, Edward felt his recent ill-humour sliding away from him, dissolving in the exhilaration of success.

'I just remembered something!' said Miranda. 'Did either of you two see the news on telly last night?'

'Not me,' said Alice. 'Why?'

'Did you see it, Edward?'

Edward shifted in his seat, suddenly uncomfortable. 'I might have.'

'I mean about the baby that was left in our park, and it disappeared, and nobody knows what happened to it.'

'It's not my baby,' said Edward, quickly.

'How do you know? Our baby was Monday, and *that* baby was Monday.'

Edward shifted again. 'It could have been a different Monday. Anyway, I know that baby's not mine because that baby was on the seat, and mine was *under* the seat.'

'The television man could have made a mistake.'

'It's not my baby,' Edward insisted.

Alice's heart began to thump. 'What did they say about it, besides it was in the park?'

'Nothing,' said Edward.

'Yes they did,' said Miranda, 'they were telling about his real mother. She's sorry she threw him away, and she wants him back.'

'Well, she can't have him,' said Edward. 'He belongs to me now. Anyway, it's not the same baby, it's a different one.'

Alice felt cold and shaky inside. This was something new to think about. She tried to think straight about this new thing, but her thoughts were a mad whirl of confusion.

The carriage was filling up. Just as the train began to move, a cheery looking woman, laden with an assortment of bags, threw herself into one of the seats across the aisle and fanned her sweaty face with her newspaper. 'Phew! Nearly missed it!' She made a noisy business of getting her breath back, grinning chummily across at the children. 'I'm treating myself to a day at the seaside,' she confided. 'Is that where you're going?'

'Yes,' said Edward, not making himself sound particularly friendly.

'Travelling on your own, then?'

'No,' said Edward.

'Anyway, is there a law against it?' said Miranda – rudely, to discourage further conversation.

'Not that I know of. It's a bit unusual though, these days. Are you all the same family?'

Edward spoke as distantly as he knew how. 'Yes.'

The cheery woman laughed. 'You must be triplets, then. Now that's something else unusual!'

'All right, it's unusual,' said Miranda. 'So what?'

'Do you know what I think?' said the cheery woman. 'I think you're bunking off school!'

Edward stood up. 'Excuse us, we have to meet our mum in another carriage.'

The woman laughed again. 'Oh yes, and I'm the Queen of Sheba!'

In the next carriage they found another pair of seats, facing one another, with only a man reading his newspaper in the seat opposite, across the aisle. Happily, Edward thumbed his nose in the direction of the cheery woman. 'Nosy old bag!'

'Nosy old Queen of Sheba!' said Miranda.

They giggled a bit, then gazed through the window as London sped by, and gave way to green fields. Miranda soon became bored with green fields. 'You know that baby, Edward . . .' she began.

'What baby?'

'You *know* – the one on the telly.'

He had been enjoying himself, and now she was spoiling it again. 'What you starting on about that for?'

'Well, it would be a bit funny, wouldn't it, if there were *two* babies left, both on the same day, in the same park.'

'Not funny at all, it's happening all the time. There's hundreds of babies get dumped. Thousands of them. *Millions* of them.'

'You're potty, Edward.'

'No, I'm not!'

'Yes you are, you're potty. I must be a bit potty myself, to come with a potty person like you!'

'I didn't ask you to come, who asked you to come?'

Edward's voice was rising. The man in the seat across the aisle turned to face the children. 'Do

169

you mind? Some of us are trying to have a quiet read.'

The children were silent for a few minutes, then Miranda began again. 'What would you do, Edward, if that *was* your baby? Would you tell Margaret to give it to its own mother?'

'No. Why should I? Anyway, it's not.'

'But if it *was*?'

'Shut up!'

'But if it was, Edward!'

'I SAID SHUT UP, ALL RIGHT?'

The passenger opposite was not just irritated now, he was angry. 'Are you kids going to be shouting like this all the way to Clappingdean? Because if so, I think I shall get the ticket inspector, or someone.'

'Don't bother,' said Edward. 'I'm not staying here anyway, I don't like the company!'

He got up, and found a seat by himself near the end of the carriage. He needed peace and quiet in any case, because he had just realised he hadn't worked out the details of how to overcome the next problem. He twisted in his seat, to gaze up and down the aisle. Then he twisted some more, hanging almost upside down, to inspect the space between his seat and the one behind.

'Look at him, Alice,' said Miranda. 'What's he doing?'

Alice said nothing.

'Looks like he's standing on his head, do you think he's lost *all* his marbles?'

Alice said nothing, again.

Miranda sighed. 'Aren't you going to talk to me, Alice? It's very boring otherwise, you know, with

170

only cows and sheep and loopy Edward to look at!'

'He's coming back,' said Alice, in her small voice.

Edward was coming back because he had seen the ticket man approaching at the far end of the next carriage along.

'Good!' said Miranda. 'About time something interesting happened!'

She followed Edward willingly back the way they had come; and, heavy with fear and misery, Alice followed Miranda.

They passed the cheery woman in the previous carriage. 'Hullo,' she greeted them. 'Haven't you found your mum yet?'

'Of course we have,' said Miranda. 'She's just coming on behind.'

Through the automatic doors, standing by the toilet, Edward instructed them. 'I've worked out how we have to do it. You know how the seats go back to back – well, we have to hide in the space between them. We have to hide in the space that's meant for the luggage.'

'People will see us going in,' Miranda objected.

'We have to find a carriage where there aren't many people. We have to find a carriage where they're all reading their newspapers, and there's some empty seats that we can hide under. Then we have to be quick.'

'Alice can't be quick,' said Miranda.

'Don't be so mean!' said Edward.

'I'm not being mean, I'm just saying Alice isn't a quick person. Alice doesn't mind me saying that, do you, Alice?'

'I'll be as quick as I can,' Alice whispered.

They passed through two more carriages, which were full. At the far end of the one after that, there were empty seats. 'We have to hide till the ticket man has gone past,' said Edward. 'Then we can come out and go back to our own seat. Easy peasy!'

'Let's hurry up and do it then,' said Miranda. 'Before the ticket man comes.'

It should have been easy enough. It *was* easy enough for Edward and Miranda. Alice saw them dive head first, each into a different space. It occurred to her they should have gone in backwards, because like that how were they going to see when the ticket man had passed? She hesitated, wondering whether to try going backwards herself – when the unplanned for, the totally disastrous thing happened!

Through the automatic doors, coming from the crowded carriage they had passed through, came four elderly women. They were laughing and joking, and one of them said, shouting the words as though one or more of her companions was deaf: '*Much* better than back there!'

'Here's a good place,' said another one, equally loudly. 'We can all be together here.'

And they sat down, two by two, right over the spaces where Edward and Miranda hid.

Alice felt sick. What should she do? She couldn't hide under a seat now – those four ladies would see her doing it. But she couldn't stay here either. The ticket man was coming. In her imagination she saw him bursting through the automatic doors,

172

bearing down on her with long menacing strides. 'Ticket please, girlie,' he would say.

And she would just stand there, helpless and guilty, a person caught breaking the law, a criminal without a ticket!

And what then?

So now I'm trapped and I can't get out, Edward thought ruefully. I shall have to stay here for as long as these people are sitting on these seats. And that may be all the way to Clappingdean!

He was dreadfully uncomfortable. He had said they should hide under the seats, but he hadn't realised that the floor would be so hard, or that there would be so little room to move. His knees and his elbows were taking the worst punishment; he tried shifting, so he would be lying on his side, but then it was the arm he was lying on that hurt. He tried easing the empty school bag round, for extra padding, but that manoeuvre was so difficult in the confined space that he gave it up.

Edward was not good at pain, and not sure how long he was going to be able to bear this for, but at least he could see a lot now. He could see a fair way the length of the train, underneath the seats.

To add to his discomfort, though, his nose was now very near to someone's smelly feet. It was an old lady's feet, Edward could tell from the shoes, and anyway they were all old ladies' voices jabbering away above him. Jabber, jabber, jabber – all about the weather, and somebody's pink knitting wool, and somebody else's bunion. If they had to talk so much, why couldn't they talk about something interesting!

Through the various legs and feet, Edward could see Miranda. That is to say, he could see a green-clad arm, and a fragment of distinctive check material, and a great deal of long blonde hair draped over a bulging school bag. Where was Alice, he wondered.

Had she managed to hide somewhere? If not, the ticket man would soon catch her, and then what would happen? Would she give it away, that she wasn't alone? She wasn't enjoying the things she had to do today, that was very clear, but she was making an effort, and that was the main thing. And she knew how to keep a secret, she'd proved that.

Of course, she wasn't a very good shape for this sort of adventure, but that wasn't her fault. People couldn't help the shape they were, it was the inside of people that mattered, not the outside. He himself, for instance, was not the handsomest person in the world, but so what? Next time Miranda said something unkind about Alice's shape he would smack her in the mouth, probably.

Somewhere deep inside him, Edward was aware of an uncomfortable feeling stirring. Alice was having a miserable time today, and it was all because of him ... Briefly, he remembered that day in the park, and how distressed she had been ... She gets upset, she gets upset, he thought ... All right, he'd make it up to her! When he got his money, he'd give some of it to Alice. Not too much, of course, just a little bit.

And *none* to Miranda.

The train was slowing, they were coming to the first stop. Edward couldn't remember how many

174

stops the board had shown, but Clappingdean was the terminus, so it would be easy to know where they must get out. They must get out where *every*one else got out. Belatedly, he hoped the girls understood this, he couldn't remember if he had explained it properly. But then, he hadn't anticipated that they would all get separated like this.

The train stopped. There was some announcement being made, somewhere, the words too indistinct to make out. Not that it mattered; the important thing was to keep still and wait for them to be on their way again.

There were footsteps, and voices. Now this carriage also was filling up. If Edward had felt trapped before, he felt doubly trapped now. How were they ever going to get out of their hiding place without being seen?

At first Miranda was happy, in her little bolt hole. This was adventure, this was fun, this was the sort of thing she'd come out to do, today. But crouching in one position minute after minute soon began to lose its appeal. It was boring, and one of her legs was going to sleep. She eased herself to lie full length on her stomach, then turned on her side quickly, and pulled her knees up to her chest, because she realised her feet must be sticking out into the aisle, and someone would surely see!

The train stopped and started again. In front of Miranda were flat granny shoes, and stockinged feet bulging with varicose veins. Miranda's nose wrinkled with distaste; she, of course, was never going to get old, ever! Behind her, coming through the noise of the train, she could hear children's voices.

'Mum, Mum!'

'Just a minute.'

'Can I have a Coke?'

'Just a *minute*.'

A different voice: 'Can *I* have a Coke, Mum?'

'Shut up the pair of you, or I'll belt you one!'

'I WANNA *COKE*!'

'Oh, all right, then.'

A pause, then two empty tins clattered to the ground. Miranda heard them rolling about behind her, imagined them spilling their last drops, staining the back of her dress. She reached behind her and grabbed one of them as it struck her thigh.

She began to calculate her chances of aiming the Coke tin through the cluster of legs in front of her, in such a way that it would strike Edward, just visible a metre or so away. She gave it a tentative push, and saw it land against one of the granny shoes. The granny shoe swung back, and obligingly kicked the tin into Miranda's face. She caught Edward's eye, grinned, and aimed the tin at him again.

Silly cow, thought Edward furiously, what does she think she's doing! He tried to grab the tin, and succeeded only in pushing it back against one of the granny shoes. 'There's something rolling around, under my seat,' a voice above complained. A brown-speckled hand appeared, waving about, trying to locate the Coke tin, which had come to rest just within Edward's reach. Cautiously, he guided the tin towards the hand.

176

The hand picked up the tin. Ha ha, Edward thought, now *that* was a clever thing I did! He cast his mind around for other clever things to do, beginning to enjoy himself, in spite of the pain. In fact, he was bearing the pain quite well, he thought, pleased with himself.

Miranda, grinning away in her own little space, made a face at him, and Edward made one back. More or less good-humouredly, the two of them settled down to a competition over who could invent the most original face.

Alice had locked herself into the toilet. She realised this wasn't the safest place to be – sooner or later someone would surely want to come in, but it was the best she could think of. Trembling, she sat on the lavatory seat and struggled to still the mad tumult going on in her head.

I'm on this train, she thought, and at this moment I can't seem to think what I'm doing here.

. . . The baby, it's about my baby! Well I *thought* he was my baby, but Margaret thought he was hers, or anyway she wanted him to be hers. Only Edward thinks the baby is his.

But he's got a real mummy as well, and I suppose he really belongs to his real mummy. And I think that *was* his real mummy on the television, whatever Edward says.

But I have to help Edward, haven't I, because of that thing Edward did for me? And I had to come anyway, because Miranda wanted me to so much, and Miranda is my best friend so I have to please her. And *that* is why I'm on this train.

It's too much to think about Harry's real mummy, it's a too big thing for me to think about.

I can only think about one thing really, and that's *how am I going to get out of this train without the ticket man catching me?*

One of the elderly ladies was fussing – the one on Edward's side, sitting by the window. She wanted her companion to let her out so she could go to the toilet. There was much rustling and scraping of granny shoes, then only three pairs of bulging legs in view.

'Occupied,' said the voice of the one who had left, coming back.

'Try another carriage,' suggested her friend.

'Oh, I'll wait. They can't be in there for ever.'

More rustling, more scraping of granny shoes, once again only three pairs of bulging legs in view. And a few moments later: '*Still* occupied. I'll have to try another carriage, like you said, what a nuisance!'

I wonder if it's Alice in there, thought Edward, suddenly.

One of the children above Miranda began to whine. 'Mum, I want to go to the toilet! *Mum,* I want to go to the toilet! MUM, I WANT TO GO TO THE TOILET!'

I hope it's *not* Alice, thought Edward.

For the fourth or fifth time, the door was being tried, and now a sharp impatient voice – muffled because of the noise of the train, but just audible: 'Come on in there, you going to be all day?' Alice

178

held her breath, and pleaded silently with the voice to go away.

Faintly, a child's whine.

A knocking. '*Is* there anyone in there?'

Again, a child's whine.

'YOU ALL RIGHT IN THERE?' The voice louder, coming right through the door.

'MUM, I WANT TO GO TO THE TOILET!'

'BELT UP, YOU!'

Inside the tiny compartment, Alice shook with fear. She felt sick and cold. How much longer could she get away with hiding in here?

The train stopped, for the second time. Station noises, footsteps, calling voices. The voice with the whining child had apparently given up, thank goodness. The train started again. Only one more stop before Clappingdean, as far as Alice could remember. If she could just hold on till they got there, if only no one else wanted to go to the toilet!

Silence for a while, except for the rattling of the train. Then once again the door was being tried.

A brief interval, then another banging on the door.

Then voices, she thought, though perhaps she was imagining that.

Again, a thumping on the door, so loud this time Alice thought someone might be trying to break it down.

Alice felt herself curling up with fear. Supposing that was what they did! Supposing someone came and broke the door down! Frantically she examined the window, wondering wildly if she could by any chance climb out – but of course she could do no such thing; even if she could get the window open, the train was going much too fast.

The knocking stopped, and the voices went away. Alice relaxed, just a little. More time passed. Perhaps they had forgotten about her . . . They *had* forgotten about her!

The train stopped at the third and last stop before Clappingdean. The usual station sounds, footsteps and voices. The train started once more. Alice began to plan what she would do when they got there. Open the door quickly, and out on to the platform. If anyone asked, she would say the door got stuck before, and she couldn't open it. They couldn't prove that wasn't true.

She was so hopeful, she almost stopped being frightened.

Edward listened to the sounds of the new arrivals in the carriage settling down.

'Where shall I put the case?'

'Shove it in there! Opposite our seat, so we can keep an eye on it.'

Edward felt something being rammed hard, against his bottom.

'I can't get it in, there's something in the way!'

'Oh, don't bother, it's only one stop. Put it in this one, behind us!'

A pause and then, coming from somewhere: 'Dad, there's somebody under the seat!'

'Where?'

'Under there, look!'

'I can't bend down that far. Read your comic. I'm trying to do this crossword!'

Alice was sickeningly aware of a new rapping on the door. 'IF THERE'S ANYONE IN THERE, PLEASE ANSWER!' The voice was not gentle, the voice was cold and menacing.

Alice's heart began to hammer, and her mouth was suddenly dry.

'WE DON'T WANT TO BREAK THE DOOR DOWN. DON'T MAKE US HAVE TO DO IT UNLESS YOU'RE ILL!' There was even more threat in the voice now. Perhaps there were terrible penalties for making the railway people break the door down. Perhaps there was a worse punishment for making the railway people break the door down, than for travelling without a ticket!

Trembling, Alice opened the door herself.

There was the ticket man, and behind him a small group of curious passengers. The refreshment woman was there too, with her trolley. 'Are you all right, love?' said the refreshment woman.

Alice forced herself to speak, but her voice sounded strange and far away in her own ears, as though someone else was saying the words, not her. 'The door got stuck. I couldn't open it.'

'Why didn't you shout, then?' said the ticket man.

'I don't know.'

'Where's your mother?'

Alice was about to say her mother was somewhere in another carriage when the thought came, not clearly but clearly enough – but why didn't my mum come and look for me, when I was stuck in the toilet all that time? She swallowed, and said nothing.

181

'Where's your mother?' said the ticket man, again.

'I'm by myself,' Alice admitted. 'There isn't a law against it, is there?'

'Let me see your ticket.'

Alice fumbled in her pocket. 'I lost it,' she whispered.

'Really? Well we shall have to have your address.'

She couldn't. Oh, she *couldn't* give her address. If she gave her address Mum and Dad would learn about all this for certain. They would be unpleased with her, they would be unpleased with her! In a panic, Alice grabbed for solution at an episode from earlier in the day.

'My aunty! My aunty's coming to meet me. At Clappingdean.'

It wasn't as good an idea as Miranda's one about Edward's grandma. Already, in her imagination Alice was hearing the ticket man demanding to be introduced to her non-existent aunty. The ticket man was holding her arm, so she couldn't run away, and he had grown big, big, bigger, till his stomach filled the width of the platform, and his head touched the sky.

She had only put it off. She had only put off the crisis till they reached Clappingdean. 'Cheer up, love, we'll be there in two minutes,' said the refreshment woman.

The train was slowing down. It'll be easy for Miranda and me to get out, Edward thought, easy peasy! They'll all be so busy with their luggage and stuff, they won't even notice us most likely. Anyway, it seems like they don't care.

182

The only worry was Alice. In the toilet? *Still* in the toilet? There was no way of knowing. He hoped she wasn't too scared. She wasn't tough, he reminded himself – not like him!

The train stopped. Now there were sounds of people moving, footsteps, voices, and the granny shoes were sliding along the floor. Hope Alice is getting out all right, Edward thought, wherever she is. He crawled backwards out of his hiding place, and stood up, stamping his feet to get the circulation back into his legs.

'Well, look at this!'

'No – I don't believe it!'

'A *stowaway*!'

'Here's another one!'

Far from not caring, the owners of the granny shoes were extremely interested, not to say delighted. Edward tried to push past, but they blocked his way, surprisingly determined – two in front, and two behind, with himself and Miranda in the middle like a sandwich.

'Better tell someone.'

'WE'VE GOT STOWAWAYS!'

Nobody came to help. 'What's the matter with everyone?' said one of the elderly ladies, disgustedly.

'Out there, on the platform, look! A guard or something, tell him!'

'Look out, don't let them go!'

Edward felt himself grabbed. He couldn't see what was happening to Miranda, but he presumed she was grabbed as well. The whole sandwich moved forward. On the platform I'll run, Edward thought. They're only old, they won't be able to hold very tight. Miranda will have to look after herself.

On the platform was the ticket man, looking fierce and grim. His hand was on the shoulder of a short dumpy girl, and that girl was Alice, looking her most wooden.

Edward was much more worried now. Not just a couple of old ladies holding him and Miranda, but the ticket man to get past, and Alice to be somehow rescued as well . . .

The sandwich stumbled on to the platform. 'Stowaways!' one of the elderly ladies announced.

'What, *more?*' said the ticket man.

Alice didn't tell, then, Edward thought fleetingly. How are we going to get out of it, though? He pointed at the sky, not too hopeful. 'Look! A UFO!'

And amazingly, they all looked!

13

Searching and searching

Edward was jubilant. Look what I did, he congratu-
lated himself, I saved us all! I'm brave and I'm
clever, and this is a wonderful day! Now everything
is going to go right, for the rest of this wonderful
day!

A glance at the station clock as he ran caused
him some slight misgiving, which he brushed
aside. Half past twelve already, well what of it? They
would just have to be quick with the rest of the
plan, that's all. Way down the road outside the
station, gulping for breath, he turned to face
the girls. 'We have to get a move on now, and
find the caravans.'

Miranda, the least out of breath of the three,
stood silent and subdued. She had been much
more frightened than she had expected to be on
this adventure. This adventure was supposed to be
fun, not being taken prisoner by a lot of horrible
old women, and nearly handed over to the railway
people to be punished, no doubt! And there was
still the return journey to be faced. Miranda
pushed that disagreeable thought to the back of
her mind.

Alice was panting too much to speak, anyway.

Edward took the girls' silence for agreement.
He stopped a passer-by to ask the way. You weren't
supposed to speak to strangers of course, because

they might want to run off with you, but who could run off with you in the middle of a busy street?

'Which caravan park do you want?' asked the passer-by, showing no signs at all of wanting to run off with Edward.

'How many are there?'

'Two – one this way, one that way.'

'Which is the nearest?'

'That way.'

That way turned out to be up a steep hill. Edward pranced ahead, full of energy and optimism. Miranda followed without enthusiasm at a distance, and Alice lagged way behind, her breath becoming more laboured with every step.

The caravan park, reached after a fifteen minute climb, was right on a cliff top. There were tents, as well as caravans, but not many people about. 'Oh, the sea, the sea!' squealed Miranda, cheering up.

Edward and Alice tramped around the site. 'Can you see them?' Edward kept asking, as though Alice needed to be reminded what they were there for. 'Can you see Margaret and Bill?'

Alice found herself distinctly relieved that she could not. Now that she was here, now it was not just a theoretical possibility, but something that might really happen at any moment, Alice was realising more and more clearly that the last thing she wanted was to come face to face with Margaret and Bill. What could she say to them? What could they say to *her*? A meeting would be painful and embarrassing – really, she could almost find it in her heart to wish this whole miserable expedition a failure.

And what about her chance of seeing Harry again? Well, what about it? To have him for just a little while, and then to lose him once more! It would hurt, it would hurt so much it would break her up like before . . . wouldn't it?

Edward and Alice joined Miranda, where she stood at the head of some winding steps. Miranda was gazing at the seashore, and the cold-looking waves washing it far below. 'Look at the lovely, lovely sea! I expect Margaret and Bill are on the beach. Don't you think Margaret and Bill will be on the beach, Alice? *I* do!' Lightly, she began to run down.

Edward followed. It did indeed seem extremely likely that Margaret and Bill would be amongst the little groups he could see dotted here and there over the sands, mostly huddling behind brightly striped windbreaks. Excitedly, Edward began to rehearse in his mind what he would say to them.

Alice plodded slowly after the other two. There was something nagging at her, something that didn't seem quite right about the caravan park they had found. Halfway down she realised what it was. 'It's the wrong sort of caravans!' she called at Edward's back; but he was too far away to hear her.

The twisty steps zig-zagged down the cliff face, the smell of seaweed tingling in Alice's nose, sharper and more pungent the further down she went. At the bottom, Alice found Edward and Miranda by the water's edge. Edward was exasperated and shouting. 'Come *on*, Miranda! We're supposed to be looking for Margaret and Bill, not paddling in the sea!'

Miranda grinned, and did a tantalising little dance in the breaking waves.

'Alice!' Edward reproached her. 'About time!'

'I'm sorry,' said Alice. 'It's the wrong sort of caravans, though.'

'What . . . ? Come on, let's leave her. Let's you and me go and look for Margaret and Bill, all right?'

'It's the wrong sort of caravans,' said Alice.

'What do you mean?'

'In this caravan park, it's the wrong sort of caravans. They're all the sort you pull along with a car. Margaret and Bill's is fixed on the ground. It's like a little house, I've seen a photo of it.'

'Oh.'

'We came to the wrong place.'

'Oh, *no!*' Edward pounded one palm with his fist, and kicked at the foam. 'Come on, then, we have to go back and find the other one . . . Come on, Miranda, we don't want to waste any more time.'

'Actually I think I'll have my swim now,' said Miranda.

'You *what?*' said Edward, with a sinking heart.

It was not a warm day. There were scudding clouds, and a light which changed minute by minute. When the sun broke through, the water glittered green and gold; when the sky darkened, the sea turned murky, and the wind whipped and stung.

'It's too cold for swimming,' Alice suggested.

'No it's not, it's boiling!'

'Why is there nobody else in, then?' said Edward. 'Come on, tell us that!'

'There *is* somebody else in – over there, look!'

Edward would very much have liked to hit Miranda. 'Leave her,' he tried. 'Let her go in and freeze to death if she wants to. You get on with freezing to death, Miranda, and we'll go and find the other caravans – all right, Alice?'

'No,' said Miranda firmly. 'Alice has to stay with me to mind my things.'

She sat on the beach, deftly removing her clothes under cover of the small towel. 'Look the other way, Edward! Why are you being so rude to look at me when I'm getting changed?'

'I'm not looking at you! Who wants to look at you? . . . Alice, come with me *please*.'

'You stay here, Alice! We can go and look for Edward's caravans after. Not that it will do any good.'

'What do you mean?' said Edward sharply. 'What do you mean it won't do any good? What do you mean by saying that?'

Miranda stood up, slim and lithe in her blue swimsuit. 'Even if you do find them, they're not going to give you the money, are they?'

'Of course they are. It was my baby, I found it.'

'But they've *got* it. Why should they pay you when they've got the baby already?'

She ran into the sea, high-stepping over the waves. When the water reached her knees she stopped running and began to wade slowly. She halted, and splashed a bit with her hands.

'With a bit of luck she'll give up,' said Edward.

'I don't think she will,' said Alice.

Miranda pushed on, creeping doggedly deeper and deeper into the grey-green sea. 'Let's leave her,' Edward tried again, but without much hope. 'Come on, Alice!'

'I can't,' said Alice, miserably. 'I'm sorry.'

Edward picked up a handful of pebbles, and began throwing them angrily into the water. All the time there had been this undefined worry at the back of his mind, and now Miranda had voiced it. It had been at the back of his mind, but so deeply buried he'd managed to avoid even looking at it, to see what it was. And now Miranda had gone and said it. Edward appealed to Alice. 'They *will* pay me, won't they? I mean, they'll *have* to pay me, it's only fair!'

Alice was silent. How could she know, any more, what Margaret and Bill were likely to do or not do? They had done one very unfair thing, what was to stop them from doing another?

Edward went on throwing stones into the sea. His face darkened with anger and frustration, as yet another cold shadow swept across the beach. He couldn't wait, he couldn't *wait*; he wanted to go *now*, to find Margaret and Bill. To get his money. To prove Miranda wrong.

There she was, stupid thing, swimming away, all by herself in that icy water. I hope she gets swept out to sea, he thought fiercely. I hope a current carries her right out, for making me wait, and saying that thing about the money ... And besides, it's getting later, and later, and later ...

Keith had come back to school for the afternoon. It was not that his mother made him, it was that he didn't want to miss PE, which was about the only lesson Keith was good at. 'Why were you away this morning?' Miss Churchwood asked him. 'Oh yes, I remember – hospital!'

'I saw Edward on the station,' Keith volunteered.

'Did you?'

'And Miranda. And Alice.'

Miss Churchwood, who had been marking the register, stopped giving Keith only half her attention, and started to give him all of it. 'Really! You mean the three of them, all together?'

'They were going to hospital too. Not the eye hospital, a different one. Edward's grandma was taking them.'

'Oh.'

It was an odd story. Miss Churchwood puzzled about it, and wondered if she should do anything about it – and eventually, temporarily, forgot it.

Miranda came out of the sea at last. 'It was lovely,' she declared. 'You don't know what you missed!'

She was blue with cold, and her teeth chattered in the sharp wind. 'It was lovely,' she insisted, again.

'Hurry up and get dressed,' said Edward.

'Why?' Miranda looked at her watch. 'It's only a quarter past one, they're only just now going back into school.'

Edward thought it must be later than that, but he said nothing. Alice was making herself be brave enough to start working it out in her head. The journey – how long had the journey taken? And school finished at half past three – how long did it take to walk home, how long before Mum began to wonder why she hadn't come? Could they possibly make it, back to Edge Hill, in time to stop her from wondering? Alice's head spun, and she felt sick, and faint.

Miranda towelled herself, and struggled with difficulty into her clothes. The manoeuvre took for ever, or so it seemed, but at last she stood shivering in her cotton dress, the goosepimples standing out on her arms as she pushed them into the thin green cardigan. 'I'm cold,' she admitted.

Alice took off her anorak. 'Here, have my coat.'

'I'm hungry as well.'

Alice produced the biscuits and bananas from her school bag, and Miranda began wolfing them down. 'Don't bother to ask if Alice wants any,' said Edward.

'Alice isn't hungry, are you, Alice?'

'Anyway, can't you eat them while we're going?'

'What's the matter with you, Edward, you are so impatient! Look!' She held out her arm. 'It's only a quarter past one!'

Distract her attention, don't let her realise! 'You'll feel warmer when we're walking,' Edward urged.

Miranda took a few steps, then stopped. 'Oh.'

'What's the matter?'

'I forgot to take my watch off when I was swimming.'

'So?'

'It's stopped. It *has* stopped! It still says a quarter past one. I wonder what the time is really.'

'It's not late,' Edward assured her quickly. 'It's not late at all.'

Miranda stood stock still, calculating. 'It could be two o'clock.'

'It's not, it's not!'

Miranda was beginning to panic. 'It could, it could! How long did it take us to get here? How long did it take us to get to Clappingdean altogether, Alice?'

'I don't know . . . I think it was a long time.'

'And we have to get back to the station, and we have to wait for the train, and then we have to go on the Underground . . . *We have to go home now!*'

'*No!*' Edward felt his insides going weak. He could see what was coming, but how to stop it? 'We have to find Margaret and Bill, you know we do!'

'Oh bother silly old Margaret and Bill! We have to go home. Before our mums find out . . . Anyway, it's my speech and drama class tonight.'

'All right, you go!' Edward shouted at her. 'You go by yourself, don't expect me to come with you!'

'I'm not going by myself, Alice is coming with me, aren't you, Alice?'

'*Alice!*' Edward pleaded. 'I *need* you!'

'Don't listen to him, Alice!'

' . . . I think it's too late anyway,' said Alice, in a half-whisper. 'It's too late to get home in time.'

Miranda was really panicky now. 'No it's not, it's not! If we hurry, it's not! Come on, Alice, let's hurry!' She seized Alice's arm and began propelling her along the beach, towards the winding cliff face steps. Edward ran, and plonked himself in front of them.

'Wait!'

'Get out of our way, Edward Lawson, you told a lie. You said we would get home before our mums find out, and we can't!'

Edward swallowed on this monstrous injustice. 'All right, I made a mistake.' It nearly choked him to say it, after Miranda's contributions to the delays, but he pressed on. 'If you go home now, though . . . If *we* go home now . . . we will have to do all that stuff on the train again. You know, the hiding . . . And on the Underground, the barriers . . . And we might really get caught this time . . .'

Miranda began to wail. 'I wish I never came!'

Edward forbore to point out that Miranda had not been invited in the first place. 'But if we find Margaret and Bill first,' he tempted her, 'it will be different.'

'How?'

'Because I will have enough money to buy tickets – for all of us, all right?'

Miranda regarded him stonily, her chest heaving. 'They aren't going to give you any money.'

'Yes, they are.'

'They aren't, are they, Alice? Edward is loopy to think they will pay him, when they have the baby already. Don't you think Edward is loopy to think that?'

'I don't know,' said Alice, honestly.

'You think they might?'

'I suppose they might. I don't know.'

The idea of a comfortable seat on the train, properly paid for, was very appealing. And if they were going to be late home anyway . . . Miranda shrugged. 'Come on, then. What are we waiting for?'

Up the cliff steps, through the caravan park,

and down the steep hill. Cold and wretched, Alice trailed behind the other two, stumbling through a nightmare, jumbled thoughts chasing one another.

I'm going to be home late, and Mum and Dad are going to know! They're going to be unpleased with me! They're going to be so unpleased with me, they might never be pleased with me again, ever.

And they'll be worried, won't they, when I don't come home from school! I know they care more about William than they do about me, but I think they'll still be worried. And I don't want my mum to be worried. Or my dad.

Will they ask the police to come and look for me?

The police.

I forgot all about the police! I forgot all about I might go to prison because I didn't take the baby to the hospital!

If the police come to find me they can find out what I did before! Oh I don't want to go to prison, I don't want to go to prison!

I'm scared, I'm scared!

And my mum's going to be worried, she *is*! I've got some money, I could phone her before she gets worried. If there was a phone box ... Only I haven't got any change because Miranda took it all for the toilet ...

Anyway I can't see a phone box. And if I go to look for one, then Edward and Miranda will get out of sight, and I shall lose them, and I will be all by myself, and anyway I can phone my mum later – there's still plenty of time for that ...

I must keep up with them, I must keep up with

195

them! Don't let Miranda and Edward get out of sight, please, please, *please* don't let Edward and Miranda get out of sight . . . !

In the middle of PE, watching Keith shin rapidly and with ease up his rope, Miss Churchwood remembered the odd story he had told, earlier that afternoon. Could it possibly be true, that Edward's grandmother had escorted three children to hospital because of some mild tummy bug?

More likely, Edward, Miranda and Alice had taken the day off for their own purposes!

. . . *Alice*, though?

Well, yes, possibly, if bossy Miranda commanded it!

She would mention it to the head teacher at playtime, Miss Churchwood decided. Mrs Rudge would decide if any action were needed.

Miss Churchwood crossed the hall to separate Flora and Leanne, who were having a loud argument about something or other.

Miranda and Edward had found a sign pointing up another hill to the other caravan park, which was called Sandy Bay. Miranda urged Edward to go faster. 'Come on, come on, you walk like a snail, do you know that?'

He was badly out of breath, trying to keep up, but not wanting to admit it. 'There's not *that* much hurry,' he told her.

'Yes there is, we have to be quick and get your money, so we can be home in time for my speech and drama, at least!'

Edward turned his head. 'Where's Alice? I can't see Alice.'

'She's slow. She's too fat to walk properly.'

'You're mean to her!'

'No I'm not. It's not my fault Alice is so fat.'

'Well, you don't have to go on about it all the time. You're not much of a friend to her really, are you? I wouldn't like to have a friend like you.'

'What do you know about friends? You haven't *got* any friends.'

'I could have if I wanted them. I could have as many as I like, if I wanted them . . . Anyway, I think we should wait for Alice. It's mean to leave her all behind.'

'Oh, don't fuss! Alice will be all right . . . Anyway, we don't really need her.'

'What do you mean?'

'Well, *I* know Margaret and Bill, don't I? *I* can tell you when we find them. And I can tell them it was you that found the baby, as well.'

'It's still mean to leave Alice.'

'Stay behind if you want to, then. I'm going on to find Margaret and Bill.'

Edward stood still, looking back the way they had come. Alice was still out of sight. He pictured her toiling up this new hill, her big red face getting redder and redder, and feeling frightened perhaps because she was all alone.

Edward stood like that for a few moments and then, not too happy with himself, turned again and broke into a run. After all, he found, he could not bear to wait one moment longer than was necessary to get his money, and prove Miranda wrong about what she said.

197

Playtime at last! Ten blissful minutes to relax in the staffroom with a nice hot cup of tea. And – oh yes, Miss Churchwood reminded herself, I must see Mrs Rudge about those three absentees.

She escorted her class to the playground.

Going down the stairs, Flora tripped because she wasn't looking where she was going. Or it might have been that Leanne pushed her, Miss Churchwood couldn't be sure. Anyway Flora tripped, and fell, bumping into Patsy as she went, and knocking her over too. Keith, in front of Patsy, managed to hold fast to the handrail and avoid being the next domino to go down.

Flora set up a wail, but it was Patsy who seemed the more hurt. She had struck her head against the handrail, and already there was a nasty egg-shaped swelling, rising above her right eye. Miss Churchwood saw the rest of her class into the playground, then took the two wounded ones to the medical room to be bathed and bandaged.

Then there was the accident book to be filled in. 'How did it happen, Flora?'

'I don't know.'

'Are you wearing slippery shoes?'

'I don't know.'

Miss Churchwood wrote 'Tripped on stairs', wishing she was entitled to write 'Pushed by Leanne', which was most likely to be the truth, she thought. Nasty piece of work, Leanne! Miss Churchwood would be extremely happy to say goodbye to Leanne, at the end of the term.

She hurried to the staffroom, for her precious cup of tea, with only two miserable minutes left for drinking it in. She had, of course, forgotten all about Alice and Miranda and Edward.

Edward and Miranda passed another sign for Sandy Bay Caravan Park, with a hand and a pointing finger beside it. 'We must be nearly there, now,' said Edward.

'Oh, *look*!' said Miranda, suddenly.

'Look at what?'

'That lady with the pram we've nearly caught up to! I'm nearly sure . . . Yes I am, I'm sure, I'm sure! *It's Margaret!*'

Edward's heart, thumping already from exertion, began to thump some more. 'Are you positive?'

'I said so, didn't I!'

The woman with the pram was big, and untidy. Her hair was done up in a sort of bun, with wispy escaped bits blowing all round it, in the wind. She wore a short pink fluffy jacket, and trousers that were covered with pink and yellow flowers – great big flowers that made her behind look even broader. The tail of a squiggly orange and purple blouse hung flapping, below the fluffy coat.

Eagerly, Edward ran three steps forward. 'No wait, wait!' said Miranda.

'What for? I can ask her for the money now!'

'*Wait*!' Miranda insisted. 'I've got a better idea. I've got a really good idea . . . Do you want to know what it is?'

'All right, what?'

14

A disastrous mistake

Excitedly, keeping at a distance, they followed the woman and her pram. Once she turned round, and Miranda dodged quickly behind Edward. 'Hide me! Hide me! It doesn't matter if she sees you, because she doesn't know you. But she mustn't recognise me until after we've done *the thing*!'

As expected, the woman turned into the caravan park. Edward and Miranda trailed her between rows of caravans much too big to be towed by any car, some even with little gardens planted around them. The woman stopped beside one of these at last, and bent over the pram as though to take the baby out.

'Oh *no!*' Miranda protested, deeply disappointed. 'She's going to take him inside – now we can't do it!'

But the door of the caravan opened, and there was a big man in the doorway – a man who waved his arms and shouted so loud the children could hear him even where they stood, six caravans along the row.

The woman left the baby and, shoulders hunched, followed the big man inside.

Edward and Miranda sprinted to cover the distance. There was a lot of noise coming from inside the caravan – voices raised, thumps and bangs, seemed like Margaret and Bill were having a good old row. Edward and Miranda stood looking down at the little pink and white face, topped by a blue woolly cap, just showing above the blankets which tucked the baby in so warmly. 'He's got bigger!' Edward marvelled.

'Well they do! Babies do, they grow . . . Go on, then, aren't you going to do it?'

Edward hesitated. It was an exciting idea, but unplanned and unprepared for. There hadn't been time to think it out – was it *really* such a good idea? Edward's heart was racing, and his knees were suddenly weak. 'Someone might see,' he muttered.

'There's nobody here. They're all on the beach. Go on, I dare you!'

'People might be looking out of their windows.'

'*Chicken*! Anyway, you keep saying it's your baby, so you've got a right to take it, haven't you?'

'I know, but – don't forget it has to be a secret. Because of the police.'

'*Chicken*!' Miranda taunted him again. 'All right, *I'll* do it!'

She took off Alice's coat, and scooped the baby out of the pram, holding it bundled in its blankets, inside the coat so that not even its head was showing. The baby began to cry, but the sound was thin and muffled. The children ran.

They ran through the rows, and out of the caravan park. They ran down the hill, and Edward wanted to go further, but Miranda said: 'It's all right, nobody's following. Nobody saw. You are such a *coward*, Edward!'

'That's not fair! I wasn't a coward on the train.

You didn't think I was a coward when I saved you from that ticket man, and those horrible old women!'

'Well, you're a coward now. Come on, let's have a look at the darling little baby.' She uncovered its head, and thrust the bundle into Edward's arms while she seated herself on the grass at the edge of the road. Then she held out her own arms. 'Come on, give him to me then . . . Oh, the angel! Oh, the little sweety!' She cuddled the baby, dropping kisses on the little pink nose, while it screamed into her face.

Edward sat down beside her. Uneasy at the way control was slipping away from him, he made a grab to retrieve it. 'You wait here then, and I'll go and get the money.'

'Oh, the dear, darling little thing . . . don't cry, don't cry . . . See, he's stopped crying . . . I thought you were going to get the money, Edward!'

'In a minute.'

'Well, hurry up, we have to be home in time for my speech and drama.'

'In a *minute*, I said. When I'm ready, all right?' It had to be done, he supposed; he just wished he felt braver. 'Oh look, here's Alice coming!'

Miranda looked up, and called to the solitary figure plodding up the hill. 'Hurry up, Alice, look what we've got!'

Alice had no breath left, and sweat was running down the heavy cheeks, in spite of the coolness of the day. She stared in bewilderment at the baby wrapped in her coat. She gulped a few times and tried to speak.

'Don't you recognise him?' said Miranda. 'We

202

found Margaret and she went in her caravan. And she left the baby in its pram outside, so we took him. She can only have him back when she pays Edward the money. Or anyway, enough money to buy the tickets for the train . . . It was my idea,' she added, proudly.

Alice's eyes were round with horror. She drew another shuddering breath, and managed to say it. '*That's not Harry!*'

'Yes it is!'

'It's not! It doesn't look like him a bit . . . And anyway, that baby's too big.'

'Well, he's grown, hasn't he?'

'He wouldn't have grown as much as that!'

Edward was furious. 'You made a mistake!' he shouted at Miranda. 'You said it was Margaret and it must not have been all the time!'

'Yes it was!' Miranda insisted. 'We saw Bill as well, didn't we? He—' She faltered. It occurred to her at that moment that she didn't actually, not *actually*, know Bill by sight at all. Margaret she had seen often, in her garden, but never Bill.

'What did he look like?' said Alice.

'Well, you know, not like anything in particular . . .'

'He had a big stomach, like a beer belly,' said Edward. 'And black hair hanging over his face.'

Alice shook her head. 'That's not Bill. Bill is thin, and he hasn't got any hair at all.'

'Funny,' said Edward bitterly. 'I thought you were going to say that. Nice one, Miranda!'

There was a stricken silence.

'You've kidnapped a baby,' whispered Alice. 'That's a crime. That's a real crime you've done!'

203

Miranda was frightened now. 'Well, I didn't know, did I? It's not my fault there was a lady that looked exactly like Margaret . . . Anyway, her *back* looked exactly like Margaret . . . It's Edward's fault! It's all Edward's fault for bringing us here in the first place!' The little speech ended in a wail. 'And I want to go *home*.'

Edward felt the world tip and turn around him. All he wanted to do was run. 'Yeah, let's go, let's go!'

'What about the baby?' said Alice.

'What about it?' Miranda unwrapped the baby from Alice's coat and laid it on the grass, where it started to cry again. Miranda stood up. 'Leave it there, it'll be all right.'

Alice was appalled. 'You can't!'

'Yes I can. Why can't I?'

'It'll get cold.'

'It's got its blankets.' Miranda was hurriedly putting on Alice's coat again.

'Somebody will find it,' said Edward. 'And look after it.'

'They might steal it,' Alice objected. She picked up the baby and cradled it protectively against her shoulder, rubbing its back to comfort it. She twisted her neck to gaze at its little blue-clad head, and Edward turned away. Seeing all that feeling made him uncomfortable – especially seeing it on Alice's face, which usually showed so little.

'Leave it, Alice!' said Miranda, frantically. 'We have to get away before anybody discovers what we did!'

'I'm going to find its mummy. Which caravan did it come from?'

'You're mad! Put it down!'

Edward had already started down the hill. He turned to call her. 'Come on, Alice! Leave the baby!'

'I'm going to find its mummy!' The first time Alice said that she hadn't been sure she meant it, but now she was. *Perfectly* sure. Whatever Miranda said, whatever Edward said.

'Go on then, *do* that mad thing!' Miranda watched Alice begin her lonely plod, up the hill towards the caravan park, then ran helter-skelter after Edward.

Edward and Miranda careered down the hill. 'We have to get to the station,' Miranda shrieked between breaths. 'We have to get out of here, we have to get back to London!'

Edward stopped, and Miranda stopped too. 'What's the matter?'

Edward was beginning, it had to be admitted, to have a distinctly poor opinion of himself. 'We can't leave Alice.'

'Yes we can.'

'We can't leave her all by herself. How will she get home, all on her own?'

'That's her problem.'

'I'm going to wait for her.'

Miranda gaped at him, then screamed: 'No, Edward, *no*! No, come on, we have to get to the station. Never mind stupid Alice, we have to get away!'

Edward regarded her with stony dislike. 'I'm staying here, all right?'

'They can be after us, though! To put us in prison or something.'

'They won't know about us. Alice won't tell.'

'They'll make her!'

'Oh, they'd make *you*!' said Edward, with heavy sarcasm. 'But Alice isn't you, is she?'

Miranda shrugged. 'Well nobody would want to be *Alice*. Come on, Edward, I don't want to go by myself. *Please*, Edward! Please pretty please with sugar on top?'

'I'm waiting for Alice,' said Edward.

'I hate you!'

'Oh, *good*!' He sat on the grass, and wriggled to make himself comfortable.

'I hope they catch you and put you in prison! Anyway, they won't catch *me*!'

Was she crying? Edward fervently hoped so, as he watched her flying down the hill.

Miranda doesn't care about Alice, she just uses her, he thought contemptuously. And she didn't care a bit about that baby. She made soppy noises over it, but that didn't mean a thing. Miranda's supposed to be pretty, but she didn't look vey pretty when she was yelling at me just now. She wasn't good to look at at all, then . . .

Not like Alice, when she was holding that baby just now . . . Actually, that was quite a good thing to look at! In a way . . .

I'd rather look at Alice than Miranda, Edward found himself thinking. Any day!

Alice was terrified.

Her heart thumped and her head swam, as she stumped along, walking deeper and deeper into the unknown, while the baby lay peaceful, and trusting, in her arms.

206

Edward and Miranda are going home without me, she thought in a panic. They're going home without me, and what is going to happen now?

I'm all by myself in this nasty seaside place, and I don't know how I'm going to get home, and I'm going to be late anyway, and my mum's going to be worried. And my dad. If I can't phone them in time.

But I have to find the *baby's* mummy!

Edward and Miranda are not pleased with me now, but I can't help that, I have to find the baby's mummy!

And the baby's mummy and daddy will ask me questions, and I won't know what to say . . .

I'll say the baby was on the grass. Well, that's true, it *was* on the grass! They can't make me say any more, if I don't want to. I found the baby on the grass, that's what I'll say.

If I put the baby down, I could run and catch up with Edward and Miranda, I could still do that, perhaps. They will be at the station, waiting for the train most likely, and I could catch up with them there.

Only I'm not going to.

I wish I never came to this place, I don't think Margaret and Bill are here at all.

And my mum's going to be worried, I think, only not yet.

Anyway, here's the caravan park!

Alice went through the big gates, and gazed up and down the deserted rows. Where to start looking? Should she just knock on one of the doors and ask if the people there had lost a baby? Her heart thumped louder. Wait a minute, wait a minute! Perhaps its parents hadn't missed it, yet. Edward and Miranda took it out of its pram, they said. If the parents were just keeping an eye on the pram out of the window, they might not have realised it was empty. Perhaps she could just put the baby into the pram, and run down the hill, and catch up with Edward and Miranda after all!

She wandered on, through the rows . . . There! That caravan way ahead, there was a pram outside that one! On wobbly knees, Alice walked towards it.

The door of the caravan opened, and a woman came out. Alice stood still. Too late to put the baby in the pram and run. What was going to happen now? The woman walked round the pram and bent over it. She *did* look a bit like Margaret from a distance, Alice could see how Miranda made that mistake.

But her voice, when she shrieked, was not in the least like Margaret's. Shrill and strident, it pierced the dead emptiness, bringing a few heads to windows. 'My baby! Somebody's taken my baby!'

A man with a beer belly appeared. '*What!*'

The woman was hysterical. 'My baby! The police! Get the police!'

That dreaded word! Paralysed with confusion and fear, Alice stood where she was, clutching the baby and trembling. A head, with shoulders and a pointing arm attached, leaned from a caravan window. 'There's your baby, that girl's got her!'

Two large bodies, hurtling towards her. Beer-belly reached her first, snatched the baby out of her arms, and gave it to the woman, who smothered its face with kisses. 'My baby! Thank Gawd, thank Gawd!'

Beer-belly towered over Alice, bellowing. 'What do you think you're doing with my son?' His face was red and bloated, and the veins stood out on his neck.

'I didn't take him,' said Alice, piteously. 'I found him and I was bringing him back.'

'A likely blooming story!'

Alice turned to run, but Beer-belly's powerful hand was round her arm, the fingers digging like pincers, into her flesh. 'Not so fast!' he said grimly. 'You've got some explaining to do, young woman!'

'I didn't take him,' Alice pleaded, again.

'Are you stopping in the Sandy Bay?'

'No.'

'You *aren't* stopping in the Sandy Bay? What you doing here in the first place, then? Eh? Eh? What you doing here?' His breath in her face smelled horrible.

Alice floundered. 'I mean *yes*.'

'Well make up your mind! Where's your mum?'

'I don't know.'

'You don't know much, do you! Show us which is your caravan, and we'll see if she's home.'

Alice began to walk. Beer-belly, still holding her arm, walked beside her. Alice tried to think, but her thinking was all frozen; there was no plan in her mind at all.

Well, she couldn't walk for ever, round and round this terrible caravan park, but what would happen if she stopped? Perhaps this dreadful man would get tired of holding her and let her go. It didn't seem likely, but the only hope she could see. Feeling more frightened with every step, Alice plodded on . . .

'We've been down this row,' said Beer-belly sarcastically. 'You're having me on, aren't you!'

Alice shook her head. She pointed at a caravan that looked suitably empty and shut up. 'That's mine,' she said, faintly.

'Right!' He dragged her to the door and hammered on it himself. No reply.

'I think my mum's gone out,' said Alice. 'She may not be back for a long time.' Surely, *surely*, he must give up now!

'Do you know what we're going to do?' said Beer-belly, with a sneering sort of grin. 'We're going back to my caravan, and I'm going to find my mobile, and I'm going to phone the police!'

Futilely, Alice began to struggle. 'No, not the police, please not the police!'

The man laughed, a deeply unpleasant laugh. 'You *did* take my baby, didn't you!'

'I didn't, I didn't, I found him on the grass!'

Beer-belly yanked her along some more. Alice remembered the money in her school bag. '*Please*, I'll give you three pounds and five p if you'll let me go!'

'Oh, will you!'

Margaret and Bill, the real ones, sat on a cliff top. They sat in Margaret's car, because that was warmer than being outside. Alice's baby was on Bill's lap. In silence, Margaret and Bill gazed at the choppy waves below them, and there was a sadness on both their faces. 'Our James!' said Bill, at last. 'Our son!'

'It's the right thing, though,' said Margaret.

Bill gave a wry little smile. 'Why has the right thing always got to be so hard, I wonder?'

'But you agree? We have decided?'

'No choice really, is there? After seeing that thing on the news!'

Margaret sighed. 'I don't suppose we could have seen it through, anyway. Look at all the problems! Things we hadn't properly worked out . . . I'm so worried you'll get depressed again, though.'

'I won't. I'll be too busy. I'll be fully stretched trying to wriggle round the strong arm of the law!'

Margaret shivered. 'Oh yes, that!'

'It's been a great three weeks though, hasn't it? *I*'ve no regrets, have you?'

'Only about Alice. I've never stopped feeling terrible about what we did to her!'

'Oh yes, poor little Alice!'

'How will we ever face her again, I wonder?' said Margaret, ruefully.

Bill spoke firmly. 'It was our last chance, Alice has got all her life. She'll have half a dozen babies of her own one day, I shouldn't wonder. And it's not as though she could have kept this one.'

'We'll keep her out of any trouble, won't we? We will do that, won't we, Bill?'

'We'll find a way,' said Bill.

Margaret leaned back in her seat and closed her eyes. She had hardly slept the night before, and now she felt totally drained. Vague dreams began to float behind her closed lids. Alice's face came and went, wearing that wooden expression which could hide, Margaret had reason to know, all the passion in the world . . .

Now that his fear was less, Edward was beginning to feel the full force of his disappointment. All that trouble, and effort, and nothing to show for it after all! His spirits sank as he contemplated the empty school bag dangling from his shoulder – the bag which should have been full of money by now.

He fidgeted, restlessly. Why hadn't Alice come back? He stood up, and peered the way she had gone. No sign of her. She surely should be back by now, it surely didn't take all that time to deliver a baby to its mother.

Were they making her tell, after all?

Well, she couldn't have told yet! If Alice had told about him and Miranda, then there would be people running to catch him, police cars with sirens screaming, all sorts!

Perhaps they were torturing her, to get the truth out of her. That man who came out of the caravan looked horrible enough for anything. Edward shivered, dismayed at where his thoughts were leading him. His heart began to knock painfully, in his chest.

Would he have to . . . ?

Should he . . . ?

Well, of course I don't *want* to, Edward thought, no one in their right mind would *want* to! The question is, do I *have* to?

Well, yes, I *do* have to! The fact is, I do have to, because if I don't I'm never going to respect myself again!

He took a deep breath, and began a jogging run up the hill.

Suddenly Margaret sat bolt upright, eyes wide open.

'We've got to go back! Now!'

Bill sighed, and gazed longingly at the sleeping baby in his lap. 'All right, I suppose it's time.'

'I don't mean back to London, I mean back to the Sandy Bay. There's something wrong.'

'Wrong with what? Wrong with the caravan?'

'I don't know!' Margaret's voice was distressed and urgent. 'I just know something's telling me we have to go back. *Now this minute!*'

Beer-belly's wife could not find his mobile. You could hear her bumbling about in the caravan looking for it, while Beer-belly kept tight hold of Alice outside. 'Get a move on!' he kept shouting at her. 'It's got to be there somewhere, use your eyes!'

A small crowd had collected to savour the drama, and keep an eye on the baby in its pram, while Beer-belly's wife searched for the mobile. One woman was certain she had been a witness to the kidnapping. 'Of course I didn't know it was a baby the girl was carrying, not at the time! You could blow me down with a feather when I realised! But I know it was that girl, I recognise the dress. And I see why she took her coat off, now! You could blow me down with a feather when I realised . . . She was with some boy.'

'It wasn't me,' said Alice. 'I found the baby on the grass, outside.'

'Save your breath!' Beer-belly sneered at her. He raised his voice to bellow at his wife again. 'Good

213

job the van's not on fire! Be burnt to a cinder time you're taking to find that mobile!'

There's nobody on my side, Alice thought in a panic. They're all against me, it's like that time in school only worse! And they're all squawking at me. Like a load of great big horrible geese, or something. Flapping their wings, and squawking at me and staring at me with their horrible cold eyes. And I'm all by myself, and there's nobody to save me!

The woman who had recognised Alice's dress was shouting excitedly. 'There he is! There's that boy!'

In the midst of Alice's terror there was something like joy. *Edward*! Someone had come to save her after all, and it was Edward! She hadn't made any mistake before, Edward was wonderful, he *was*. She opened her mouth and breathed his name.

'See? She knows him!'

Edward felt highly pleased with himself as he ran towards the crowd which was torturing Alice to make her tell. How noble he was being – quite heroic, in fact! How shaming if it had gone the other way, and he had let himself be too scared to come back! His feet skimmed the ground; carried along on a surge of elation he was almost looking forward to having dreadful things done to him, if such was to be the price for saving Alice. He could take it! No one was going to call *him* a coward!

As soon as he was near enough to be heard, he began to shout. 'You can let her go! I was the one that took the baby!'

'No you weren't,' asserted one of the bystanders.

'You were the one that was with her. *She* was the one that took him!'

They didn't all rush at him, as he had expected, and pin his arms behind his back, and frogmarch him to the police station. They hardly seemed interested in him at all. Edward felt the elation fizz out of him, like a balloon that's been punctured and gone off pop.

What was happening, then?

Oh, disaster, they weren't torturing Alice to make her tell, they were *accusing* her! 'No, no, you've got it wrong! It was me and . . . another girl,' he finished, lamely.

'You silly little prat,' said the man with the beer belly. 'Who's going to believe that? This lady here recognised her dress!'

They weren't going to let Alice go. He had confessed, he had done his noble bit, and they still weren't going to let her go! Nonplussed, Edward stood deflated for a minute, then pointed to the sky.

'Look,' he shouted, 'there's a UFO!'

No one took the slightest notice.

Bill drove Margaret's little red car through the gates of the Sandy Bay Caravan Park. 'Can't see any smoke anyway,' he said. 'Or fire engines, or police cars.'

'I've still got that feeling,' said Margaret.

'Oh, you and your feeling! I reckon it was just a dream you had!'

'Look!' said Margaret. 'What's going on up there?'

'Nothing much. Some bloke, holding a kid by the arm, and a few gawpers.'

Suddenly Margaret turned very white. 'It's *Alice!*'

'Come on – it can't be! What's she doing here?'

Margaret was shaking now, her heart pounding. 'Drive nearer!'

The little red car approached the small crowd. Bill whistled through his teeth. 'My God, you're right!' He slowed down and braked.

'She's in trouble! I knew it, I knew there would be *something!*' Trembling with anxiety, Margaret released her seat belt and flung open the door.

'Stay here!' said Bill, sharply. 'Looks like a nasty customer. I'll deal with it!'

There was a small crowd, and a man with a beer belly gripping Alice, and an unknown boy who kept insisting that Alice didn't do it, only no one seemed to be listening to him. 'Didn't do what?' Bill demanded. 'What's she supposed to have done?'

'Bill!' Alice called. 'Help me!'

So they *were* here, Edward thought in momentary triumph. They were here all the time, like I thought!

Beer-belly glared at Bill. 'Who are you?'

'Don't worry, Alice, I'm here now! What's she supposed to have done?' Bill repeated.

'Pinched this gentleman's baby, out of its pram, would you believe?' said an indignant voice. 'Terrible thing, innit? Don't know what kids are coming to, these days, honestly you could blow me down with a feather!'

'I didn't do it!' said Alice, desperately.

'She didn't, she didn't!' said the boy.

216

'You heard them,' said Bill to Beer-belly. 'She didn't do it. So let her go!'

Beer-belly snorted, contemptuously. 'I don't know who you think you are, but I'm getting the police.' He jerked his free elbow in the direction of Edward. 'For that little scumbag as well, he was in it! Haven't you found that mobile *yet?*' he bawled at his wife.

'Have you looked in your pocket, by any chance?' she bawled at *him*, through the caravan window.

'It's not *in* my pocket, woman! I'd know if it was in my pocket, wouldn't I?' He fumbled with his free hand. 'Oh well, how am I supposed to remember everything, with all this going on! OK, OK, I've got it now, save your bitching . . . See if I can dial 999 with me nose!'

'I wouldn't do that if I were you,' said Bill. 'Not unless you want to end up on a charge.'

'What you on about?'

'Assault.' said Bill.

'What assault? I haven't assaulted nobody.'

'You've assaulted this young girl. Holding her like that is assault. And you can be put on a charge for it.' Bill was not totally sure of his ground here, so he invented an extra bit. 'Her father is a magistrate, you may be interested to know.'

Beer-belly scowled, and released Alice as though she had suddenly become red hot to the touch. She ran to Bill and gripped his arm, burying her face against his shoulder.

'Of course,' Bill pressed on, 'her father may have you put on a charge anyway. Whether you call the police or not.'

217

Beer-belly stood in angry silence, taking this in. His breathing was fast, and the veins on his neck stood out alarmingly.

'It's all for the criminal these days,' he shouted at last. 'Decent law-abiding people get blamed for everything, and the criminals get away with it!'

'I *know*,' said Bill, grinning. 'It's a very unfair world.'

Beer-belly turned, climbed into his caravan and banged the door. The little crowd muttered and buzzed, disappointed at the way all the excitement had suddenly fizzled out. 'They shouldn't get away with it!' someone called. Edward backed warily, and retreated to a position behind the little red car. What was going to happen to *him* now?

'Come on, Alice,' said Bill. 'Margaret's waiting.'

Alice felt dizzy. Her knees trembled so much, if she didn't hold on to Bill she might fall down, she thought. Her relief and gratitude were so enormous there was no room at that moment for any other feelings. Whatever Bill and Margaret had done in the past she would gladly forgive them. 'You saved me!' she whispered.

Edward heard the words, and it was like being trodden on – squashed to the ground by somebody's boot. Bill had been the one to save Alice – Bill, not Edward. All *he* had succeeded in doing was making a fool of himself, Edward thought, bitterly. Nice one, Edward! Oh, *nice* one!

A woman had got out of the car, and was hugging Alice, which was a soppy and embarrassing thing to look at. Edward peered through the back window. Strapped to the seat was a carry-cot, with a sleeping baby in it. *His* baby! Edward's spirits rose. 'You owe me a thousand pounds,' he said to Bill.

'You what?'

'It's my baby you know, I found it. All right, five hundred.'

Bill laughed. 'My dear lad, at this moment I doubt I could put my hand on fifty! And anyway, we're not keeping the baby. We're taking him back to his real mother.'

15

Twists and turns and a few surprises

Margaret stopped hugging Alice, and reached into the car. Gently, she lifted the baby out of his carry-cot, and put him into Alice's wondering arms. He had grown, and in only two weeks his face had changed – filled out – but Alice would have known him anywhere, she thought.

Her Harry!

'I'm sorry, Alice,' Margaret was saying. 'I'm so, *so* sorry for what I did to you. There just didn't seem to be any choice.'

Alice hardly heard her. She put her cheek against Harry's, and felt his warm breath on her skin. He stirred in his sleep, and Alice's heart turned over. Her throat was so full she could barely speak, but she managed to murmur the words: 'I love you, oh I *love* you!'

'Come on,' said Bill. 'Let's get in the car and get away from here.' There was a lot still unexplained – how these kids got here, for instance, and what was the real story, about the baby taken from its pram. But explanations could wait. There would be plenty of time for explanations.

They all piled in.

Suddenly fear gripped Alice once again. 'Will I go to prison after all, then?' she asked, anxiously.

'No, no!' said Margaret. 'That was never going to happen! I'm sorry I let you believe it might. I was afraid to reassure you too much, I didn't really know *what* to say. I'm so sorry, Alice – please will you forgive me?'

'Won't there be trouble, though? When you take the baby back? I mean, yes, I think it's right for him to go back to his real mummy, but won't the police have to know about me so I will be in trouble?'

'You won't be in any bad trouble. We'll keep you out of it altogether if we can; but anyway Bill and I are going to take all the blame. Don't worry, Alice, no one is going to do anything terrrible to you because of this, I promise!'

Relief washed over Alice like a warm, healing stream. Then she remembered something. 'I told a lie too, you know,' she confessed. 'I said nobody knew about the baby except me and they did. Edward knew, and Miranda knew. So I did a bad thing to you, as well.'

'How about we all just forgive each other?' Bill suggested. 'And start again!'

'*Yes*,' said Alice, warmly. 'Let's all do that!'

She was happy. The topsy-turvy world she had been living in had somehow sorted itself out – all its pieces back in their right place, or so it seemed. True, she was losing Harry again, but never mind; for these few moments, she could sit on the back seat of Margaret's car – touching her baby, stroking his soft little cheek, aware that there had to be a future, but only the *now* quite real.

Until Margaret spoke again.

'We must let your parents know you're safe, though. They'll be going out of their minds with worry.'

Dismay and guilt came down like a dark cloud. Of course, of course, how could she have forgotten? 'What's the time?' Alice asked, her heart beginning to race once more.

Bill looked at his watch. 'Two minutes after half past three.'

Alice's heart slowed, just a little. 'It's all right, they won't have missed us yet. They'll think we're just coming out of school.'

They were driving down the hill towards the town.

'What about Miranda?' said Alice, remembering. 'Miranda came with us too, you know, Margaret. What happened to her, Edward?'

Edward, squashed uncomfortably close to Alice, and brooding wretchedly, hardly heard her. Everything had gone wrong for him, hadn't it? He was sick of it all now – sick of failure, and disappointment, and this adventure which had come to nothing in the end. Out of the blue the thought came – *I want my grandma!* I want to be home, with my grandma! Only I was horrible to her, wasn't I? I was horrible to her, I hate myself!

'Where's Miranda, Edward?' said Alice, again.

Edward shrugged. Miranda? Who cared what happened to that useless waste of space? 'I expect a Stranger got her by now,' he said with some satisfaction. 'And serve her right!'

'Look for this Miranda first then, I suppose,' said Bill.

Miss Churchwood dismissed her class, and made for Mrs Rudge's office. Would there be much point in phoning the parents now? But yes! If there really

222

was something wrong, it could be very important for Miss Churchwood to tell what she knew. Supposing those three children had decided to run away from home? Or just to have a day out in town? Anything could happen! And a whole afternoon wasted when the police could have been looking for them!

Mrs Rudge looked up, as Miss Churchwood entered. 'Ah, Miss Churchwood, I was wanting a word with you. What can you tell me about Leanne? I've had Flora's mother up this afternoon. Very concerned, says Flora's getting scared to come to school because Leanne keeps picking on her.'

'Why doesn't that surprise me?' said Miss Churchwood, bitterly.

'Of course, whatever we do will have to be done tactfully. Flora mustn't know her mother's been to see me. She'd run away, apparently, if anyone suspected she'd told on Leanne. Her mother had to prise it out of her with a crowbar, last night.'

Miss Churchwood and Mrs Rudge discussed the problem of Leanne at length. It was quite ten minutes before Miss Churchwood remembered why she had gone to the office in the first place.

Edward grudgingly suggested that Miranda might be at the station, since they had come by train in the first place. 'We can phone from there,' said Margaret. But Miranda was not at the station, and she couldn't have got on a train because there hadn't been one.

'She's probably been abducted by aliens,' said Edward. 'Anyway, I hope so.'

'What's the time now?' said Alice, anxiously.

223

'Just twenty minutes to four,' said Bill. 'We could give it another five, couldn't we?'

Alice, holding the baby once more, was getting distraught. 'Can't we phone my mum first?'

'There seems to be only one phone in this station,' said Margaret. 'Go on then, Alice, you first! Come on, you'll have to give me James – I mean Harry – while you do it.'

Alice hesitated, suddenly nervous. 'What shall I tell her?' she whispered.

'Just say you're safe, and with me,' said Margaret. 'That's the important thing, isn't it!'

Alice dialled, and waited, and dialled again. 'I can't get through,' she wailed. 'My mum's on the phone to somebody else.'

'Alice Cousins' line's engaged,' said Miss Churchwood.

'And Miranda's?'

' . . . No answer.'

'What about Edward Lawson?'

' . . . Engaged as well.'

'We'll try again later. There are one or two others of your class I was wanting a word about, while you're here . . .'

'I'm sorry I was a pig to you, Grandma,' said Edward. 'I'm really, really sorry! And I'm sorry I did this naughty thing today. I'm really, *really* sorry.'

'Edward, I'm glad you're sorry, but I really don't need to hear you say it another five hundred times. The important thing is you're safe, thank God or whatever, and someone sensible is bringing you

224

home. What about the girls? Has someone told *their* parents?'

'Alice couldn't get through to her mum,' said Edward.

'And Miranda?'

'Oh, the same thing, I think.' Edward couldn't be bothered to mention that Miranda was still missing. *Grandma!* Grandma was waiting for him, not ranting on about what he had done, or making any sort of fuss – just loving him . . . Like always! And how come he'd never appreciated that properly before?

Miranda? Miranda wasn't worth wasting breath on. Anyway, if she wasn't found yet she would be soon, so what was the difference?

'I'll go round then, shall I?' Grandma was saying. 'You give me Alice's address, or Miranda's, then I can go and tell them what's happened, and nobody needs to worry any more.'

Oh, Grandma, Edward thought fervently, you are the best!

'Sorry to bother you,' said Miranda's mother to Alice's mother. 'Your line was engaged, and I was hoping to catch my daughter. It's her speech and drama class tonight, and I'm not sure if the scatty thing's remembered.'

'They're not back from school yet.'

'Oh – well they can't be much longer. Do you mind if I wait a few minutes?'

'Oh, *do!*' Alice's mother was missing Margaret, who had never been a close friend, but a welcome bit of company now and again. 'You're always so busy, aren't you? We don't seem to have had any chance to get to know each other!' She had been chatting to her sister, and had quite forgotten that she had left the phone lying, the line open and useless, while she made this new friend welcome.

'I've been wanting to say how glad I am Miranda's teamed up with your girl,' Miranda's mother said, warmly. 'She's such a sensible, reliable kid. Kind, as well. You don't know how I envy you sometimes!'

'*Really?*' said Alice's mother, surprised. 'Ho, hum!'

Bill thought Margaret and the children should spread out along the High Street and look in all the shops while he stayed in the car with the baby. It was Alice who found Miranda, clutching an ice cream, and sobbing her heart out with fear. She had taken shelter in Woolworths, where there were a lot of people, and a good chance of not being noticed.

'It's all right,' Alice comforted her. 'We're going to get home all right – Margaret and Bill are going to take us. Actually I think Bill and Edward are going by train, because there isn't room for all of us in the car.'

Miranda allowed herself to be led into the street, where they met Edward, at whom she launched a stream of abuse.

'You great stupid ugly thing!' Miranda stormed. 'You made me lose my coat, and miss my speech and drama, and everything. I wish I never met you, actually I wish you were never born!'

Edward shrugged, ignoring the tiresome cow.

Alice was silent for a moment. All of a sudden

she was seeing Miranda with new eyes – clear eyes that no longer liked very much what they saw. Then she said, in her quiet voice: 'That's not a nice thing to say, Miranda, and you shouldn't say it. Edward *isn't* ugly for one thing. And he is also the bravest person I know. Seeing he came back for me when he didn't have to . . . And I think that was wonderful, actually, only you're too selfish to understand, aren't you? I'm sorry.'

Edward looked the other way, because it was embarrassing to hear yourself being praised like that. All the same, from feeling distinctly shrunk and diminished, in his mind he was suddenly six centimetres taller.

Why, it hadn't been such a bad day after all!

'No, no, I won't stay,' said Edward's grandma, to Alice's mother. 'Just came round to let you know the girls are safe.'

Grandma's news had been a shock. Miranda's mother was only just now beginning to take it in. 'We were thinking of ringing the school,' she said. 'The police would have been next. Just wait till I get my hands on that little madam!'

'Ah well,' said Grandma comfortably. 'You know what kids are like! Up to high jinks all the time. But no harm done, and as I said, someone called Margaret is bringing them home.'

She had a shrewd idea there was more to that adventure than high jinks, and she might or might not ever learn all the facts. What she was chiefly concerned about, right at that moment, was how to keep the peace now between Edward and the father he had never really got on with.

227

Now she knew that Alice was on her way home, and there was nothing serious to worry about, Alice's mother was rather beginning to enjoy herself. 'There's a mystery about Margaret, you know,' she commented to Miranda's mother. 'I can't wait to find out what it is!'

Edward's grandma hurried home, where the phone was ringing and ringing.

'Oh yes, it's quite true,' she assured a worried Miss Churchwood. 'I've been looking after them all day. They're all right now – back at school tomorrow I shouldn't wonder . . . No, no, of course I don't mind you ringing. I suppose it did seem an odd sort of story but there it is . . . Sorry I haven't time to talk any more just now, goodbye!'

Grandma's little monkey face creased in a gleeful grin. Don't suppose the woman believed me for a minute, she thought, but she can't very well come out with it and call me a liar, can she?

And it was only a *little* fib!

No reason for that school to know anything more than they had to. Whatever was really behind this escapade, Grandma was prepared to protect Edward with her life if need be.

Funny how the stars were right about today, though, she thought. 'An unwelcome surprise in the evening.' Let them all jeer, the stars weren't such rubbish as people liked to make out!

Emily's mother watched Emily cuddling her baby, and thought of the sacrifices *she* was going to have to make. Give up her job, for one thing – *someone* had to look after the baby while Emily went to school. Oh well, making sacrifices was what mothers were for, Emily's mother thought.

'What are you going to call him, then?' she asked, cheerfully.

'I haven't decided. I can't really think about anything except how happy I am.'

Later on Emily would be properly grateful to her parents. Later on, Emily would truly appreciate how much she owed them. She was only fifteen and three-quarters, after all, and she still had a lot of growing up to do.

As far as the children were concerned, Bill had been very determined about playing down the story. All that had been necessary for Emily and the police to know was that a boy called Edward had found the baby, and a girl called Alice had looked after him for a day. And there was another girl called Miranda, who had been mixed up in it as well. That had been naughty, of course, but the real criminals had been himself and his wife. They were the adults, and they should have known better, and if anyone was to be punished, in any way at all, it should be them!

Emily had wept and begged that *no* one should be punished. 'They *loved* him,' she implored. 'They took care of him and they brought him back to me in the end! I don't want anybody to be in trouble, for doing what I should have done, all the time!'

And Emily got her way.

'What are you going to wear?' Miranda enquired, excitedly.

'I don't know,' said Alice. 'I haven't thought about that.'

The girls were in Alice's playhouse, like the old days. Today, however, they had something new and special to discuss. That morning, totally unexpected, had arrived invitations for each of them to Emily's baby's christening!

Alice's heart fluttered with joy. She was going to see Harry again, *she was going to see Harry*! Of course, she supposed she mustn't go on thinking of him as Harry, though that was going to be one of his names ...

There was another reason Alice had to be happy, only that must be a secret for now. 'Things can go wrong,' Margaret had warned her. 'So it's best if we don't tell everyone just yet. But oh, Alice, I have to tell *someone*, or I think I'll just burst. The thing is, *it looks like I'm going to be lucky after all!*'

Margaret was growing a baby! Margaret and Bill were going to have a baby of their very own, how wonderful!

Alice would have liked to be able to share the good news with Miranda, but then she thought Miranda probably wouldn't be interested anyway. She made an effort to tune in to Miranda's thinking. 'What are *you* going to wear, then?'

'I'm going to ask my mum to buy me something new ... Oh, look who's coming down the path! Your darling Edward – I suppose he's got an invitation as well!'

The girls were at a new school now, Edward at a different one; life had moved on. The gardens were splashed with red and gold, and the smell of autumn hung sharp with new promise, in the early-fading October afternoon.

Edward burst into the playhouse, waving his invitation triumphantly. 'What have you come for?' Miranda complained. 'Why couldn't you just phone, like you're always doing? Like you and Alice are girlfriend and boyfriend or something!'

'Is there some law says I can't come my own self if I want to? Look, Emily's calling the baby after *me*! Edward Harry James, but my name is the first! Because I was the one who found him!'

Miranda snorted. 'Emily wouldn't be so pleased with you if she knew you were going to sell her baby! I bet she wouldn't be so pleased if she knew about that!'

'*And you're not going to tell her!*' said Alice, firmly. 'Because if you do I'm never going to be your friend again. *Ever.*'

She gave Edward a small shy smile, and Edward thought, pity Alice is too kind to just dump Miranda anyway, and have done with it! And then he thought, no I don't mean that, I don't mean that, I wouldn't want Alice to be any different than she is . . .

He gazed with pleasure at his invitation. Perhaps, after all, he would like to have a baby of his own one day. Perhaps he would change his mind about not wanting to get married. One day. *After* becoming a millionaire, of course!

When the others had gone, Alice went into a delightful private dream. She dreamed that Emily would let her go on seeing Harry, watch him growing into a toddler, and then a real little boy going to school. Perhaps Emily would let her take him out sometimes – Alice would be a big girl herself, by then. One day she might tell him the story of how she looked after him for a while, when he was tiny . . .

But no, no, *that* wouldn't do, would it? Emily wouldn't want Harry to know she'd abandoned him, when he was just born, and Alice wouldn't want him to know that either. He wouldn't understand. Alice only half understood it herself.

No, that was probably one secret that must be kept for ever.

Walkinstown Branch Tel. 4558159

The Runaways

RUTH THOMAS

Winner of the Guardian Children's Fiction Award

Julia and Nathan have no friends to speak of. They're the misfits of Mrs Henrey's class – always the last to be picked for the team, and always without a partner. Until they discover a stash of money in a deserted house and suddenly, instant popularity seems just around the corner.

But so is trouble, in the shape of the adults who start asking difficult questions. There is only one thing the pair can do now, and that is to run away!

'A first rate novel.'
Guardian

'A fast-moving and totally absorbing adventure story.'
Books for Keeps

RED FOX £4.99   0 09 959660 1